STALKING THEIR MATE

PERFECT PAIRS
BOOK TWO

TAMSIN BAKER

AMELIA SHAW

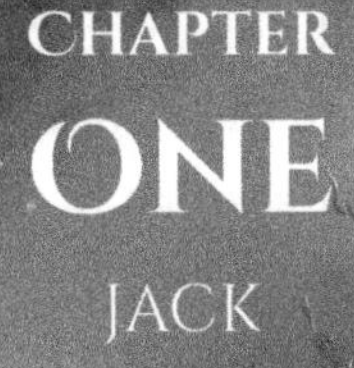

CHAPTER
ONE

JACK

"Laura, Brandon, and Tyler, you are now bonded for life." The elder officiating the service for my cousins stood beneath an archway the family had erected in my aunt and uncle's backyard.

I grinned and whooped, happiness for the couple in front of me flowing through my blood like rich wine, giving me a sense of warmth and satisfaction.

Though, was it still a couple if there were three of them? *I guess not.*

I hadn't worried about what to call them before now. Despite the existence of perfect pairs, we didn't have many ménage relationships in our family.

A throuple, maybe?

Laura, the bride, lifted her face toward her two men.

Brandon, my big cousin, pressed his lips to his mate's. Then Tyler, his twin brother, turned their woman toward him, cupping her face and kissing her in turn.

A quiver of pain pierced the happiness within my chest, like a needle sliding through a balloon, deflating the joy. Such a small thing to witness, but oh-so-powerful. The image before me was like a dream. What my brother, Scott, and I should have had.

We were a perfect pair too, just like Tyler and Brandon. But we were fifteen years older that our younger cousins. We should have already found our fated woman and mated her long before now.

But we'd both chosen a different path.

In retrospect, we'd chosen the wrong path.

Watching Brandon, Tyler and Laura together made me ache with yearning for what might have been. I swallowed hard, trying to dislodge the deep-seated feeling.

Scott, who stood beside me and clearly sensed my mood, jammed his elbow into my side. Pain spread through my ribs.

"Don't you dare go all maudlin on me today," he said in a low voice.

I scowled, leaned forward, and hit my brother with a swing of my shoulder. "Why the hell would I do that?"

Scott chuckled and lay his arm across the back of my plastic garden chair. "Because I know you still think she's out there. Some perfect woman made just for us." He huffed out a laugh, but there was no humor there. "But you know that won't happen now. We're pushing fifty, Jack. We're done."

I turned and glared at him. He needed to get over all the crap his wife had put him through and move forward.

"You might be done, but I'm not," I said.

Age is a number. Nothing more.

I looked back toward the newly bonded family, taking quick breaths through my nose to calm down. My heart pounded heavily with anger, and I shouldn't feel that way at a bonding ceremony.

After the ceremony, Scott and I mingled with the other guests. I enjoyed the light hearted banter and general good feelings of being with my family.

When we stopped to get another drink, I scanned the area and watched Laura bounce from one relative to another.

I shook my head with a chuckle.

Poor woman didn't know what she was in for, with our family. We were loud, and big and boisterous. My gaze drifted around the crowd until it fell upon a beautiful woman standing by the refreshment tables.

I blinked as lust punched me in the gut.My hungry gaze devoured the woman. She had shoulder length reddish-brown hair and a beautiful face currently set in a sad expression. Her body curved in all the right places, yet her silver-gray slip dress hid most of her flesh from sight.

I nudged Scott and nodded in her direction. "Who is *that*?"

Scott turned to stand shoulder-to-shoulder with me, peering in the direction I indicated. "You mean the woman with…" He let out a small groan and stumbled until he grabbed the back of a chair.

I stared at my brother in shock. He felt the pull, too? We'd been told by other family members that our fated mate would create a strong feeling inside us, and perhaps even be quite shocking. Almost painful at first.

Looks like they hadn't exaggerated.

Thank you, God! We've found her.

"Quick, we need to get to her." I slapped my brother on the back.

He growled at me. "Calm down, Jack. We can't just rush over there. I don't think she has any shifter in her, so she must be from Laura's side."

I nodded, excitement building in me like a running faucet in a bathtub, filling me up to overflowing. I couldn't wait for the moment when we could finally connect with our true mate. But first, we had to confirm that she really was what we thought she was.

"Okay, so we should talk to Laura first," I said. "Ask for an introduction."

I grinned at Scott, a strange feeling flowed between us, a sizzling connection and a joined purpose. I hadn't felt that with him since we were teenagers. Before we'd met our wives and been torn apart.

Scott led the way through the thick crowd, and I followed. My breath caught in my throat. I couldn't stop my gaze from darting over to the woman with the auburn hair and I copped another punch of recognition to my gut. Something told me—*demanded*, in fact—that I not ignore her.

God, this odd pain was a good feeling after so long waiting to meet 'the one'.

Alive, I suddenly realized. I felt alive, where before I'd felt like I was merely existing.

We found Laura collapsed on a garden chair, panting with the stress of being thrown from one set of arms to another.

I stepped in front of her and smiled down at the woman who had made my cousins so incredibly happy. "Laura, you look absolutely beautiful."

And she did.

Her hair was swept up in a fashion that was both feminine and suited her face. The twin bite marks on her exposed shoulders were visible, and looked recent. I suppressed the shifter rumble that passed through me.

One day, Scott and I would mark our mate like that, too.

Laura looked up and smiled at us. "Wow, you two look amazing."

I grinned and inclined my head. "Thanks."

My gaze strayed back to where the woman in silver stood eating one of the pastries that adorned the table. I forced my attention back to Laura. It was a struggle, though.

The other woman's pull was magnetic, and I clenched my jaw to stop from turning back.

Laura sat up straighter and glanced in the same direction, a puzzled look on her face. "What are you two staring at so intensely?"

She put out a hand and I lifted her off the chair, steadying her as she wobbled.

"Oh, that's better." She adjusted her white dress, which looked like it had some sort of corset thing underneath. It gave her a lovely hourglass shape, but I wasn't sure how comfortable it would be.

"Laura, who is the woman in the silver dress?" Scott asked.

Laura's eyes widened, and then she turned and scanned the area while I held my breath. "Oh, she came!"

She clapped her hands and took a step in that direction.

Scott's hand shot out as quickly as a rattlesnake and stopped her in her tracks. "Is she a friend of yours, Laura?"

His voice was deeper than usual now. I'd never heard him sound like that before. He had always put up a strong front when it came to the subject of our fated mate. He'd been adamant that he wouldn't even want her if she finally did show up, but that was all it was.

A front.

Yes, brother. We've found her. I haven't even touched her, yet I can feel her drawing me in. You can too, and I know you're probably terrified, but don't be!

Laura cocked her head and stared at Scott.

"She's my cousin from up north. I invited her to our church wedding that I'd organised for my human family, but she couldn't come that day. So, I told her about today and changed the time on her invitation so she'd arrive late and miss the ceremony itself. Though..." She tapped her foot and pulled her arm out of Scott's grip. "I won't be upset if she knows that I'm mated to both Tyler *and* Brandon. My family will work it out eventually."

Ah, I'd forgotten about that complication. Non-shifters didn't understand the bond that could form between three people like we did.

My stomach flickered and I ground my teeth. Back to the issue at hand.

"Can you introduce us?"

I needed to touch Laura's cousin to confirm whether she really was *our woman*—or not.

But in my heart, I already knew she was mine. And my brother's. She was *ours*.

"Sure..." Laura sashayed through the throng of people and made her way to the woman's side.

Scott and I followed more slowly in her wake.

Excitement rose within my belly and I was reminded of the year I'd turned fourteen and went on my first date. In fact, I was probably *less* nervous back then.

"You came!" Laura cried as she threw her arms around the woman, who laughed and hugged her back.

Come on, come on.

Laura pulled back and stared at her cousin with a concerned frown. "I don't mean to be rude, but... you look like shit, Ash."

I frowned at Laura. That wasn't a nice thing to say to her cousin, let alone a woman that beautiful.

My balls tightened as I took my time admiring her voluptuous figure. I usually dated women who were ultra-fit and trained hard to minimize their body fat.

Studying her, I was instantly converted to lusting after women with fuller figures. I'd never noticed how incredible bigger breasts could be, or how lush hips should be admired, not exercised into nonexistence.

I'd never look at a woman's body the same way again.

Ash sighed. "Thanks, sweetie, I know. Whereas you look fantastic."

Laura did a twirl and stuck her hip out at an angle. Cheeky woman. "Why thank you, darling. The love of a good man...and all that."

Ash quirked an eyebrow at Laura. "Or men, perhaps?"

Laura blushed a pretty pink and stared at Ash, her mouth tugging down. "Yeah...well..."

Ash smiled at Laura with genuine warmth and love. "As long as you're happy, honey."

Next to me, Scott shifted from foot to foot.

Laura whirled around, seemingly just remembering that we were standing there waiting. "Oh, Ash, let me introduce you to Brandon and Tyler's cousins. It's common in their family for men to be born into nonidentical twin sets. This is Scott and Jack. Guys, this is my cousin, Ashleigh."

I stepped forward with Scott beside me, my back ramrod straight as I stared at Ashleigh.

Her smiling face froze, before her mouth pulled down on both sides.

"Nice to meet you gentlemen," she said, but her tone was like ice. I wasn't deterred. Whatever her baggage, we would cope. God knew we had enough of our own.

I stuck my hand out at the same time as Scott. I would have laughed at the comedy of it all if the moment hadn't been so serious for us.

This is it.

With this first touch, we would know if Ashleigh was the woman we'd waited twenty-five years for.

She looked at our hands and her nose wrinkled up in seeming distaste. Neither of us dropped our arms away.

No fucking way are we backing down, beautiful. Pick one. Touch us.

Finally, Ashleigh sighed as if she realized we weren't budging. She reached out to shake Scott's hand first.

Having to watch it happen rather than being the first one to experience it, hit me in the gut with disappointment.

But even so, I didn't dare blink, in case I missed something.

As her hand connected with his, she gasped and her face reddened.

Then she crumpled and sunk toward the ground.

Instinctively I jumped forward to catch her, and electricity shot through my body as we connected. Tingling pain pulsed straight through my arms and into my core. My body weakened, and I almost hit the dirt myself.

I groaned in unison with Ashleigh as she dropped Scott's hand to cling to my arms.

I forced all of my strength into my legs and locked my knees while pure pleasure replaced the electrical pain. Like a cleansing white light, it slid through my chest and down my arms and legs.

She's ours.

She stared up at me from the circle of my arms, her blue eyes shocked and vulnerable. Her lips parted as she took a breath, and I fought the urge to lean down and kiss her.

My heart thumped in my chest, and my cock stirred in my suit pants.

As if she could sense my desire, she began to struggle, her eyebrows lowering as her mouth took on an angry tilt. I reluctantly let go of her solid warmth.

She staggered toward Laura and grabbed hold of her cousin like a life raft.

My arms still tingled like I'd lifted weights for too long, yet I yearned to have her back and pressed against me, no matter the cost.

"What the fuck was that?" Ash spat the words at us.

I bristled and lifted my hand to signal that everything was okay. Several male cousins around me growled in warning. They could feel theh vibrating emotions that threatened to overflow, and no one wanted to shift amongst mixed company.

They didn't need to worry. I was in full control of my mountain lion despite the circumstance. I'd had so many years of practice shoving that side of me down when I needed to.

I shared a look with Scott, and then stared back at Ashleigh. What was the next step?

"Ash, how long are you here for?" Laura asked, as if sensing our indecision about how to proceed.

Ash stopped staring at me and Scott like we'd committed some sort of crime.

Which we hadn't.

"Uh, a week or so," she said. "I took some leave."

Hell, yes!

We had time to convince her to stay.

Laura beamed. "Brilliant. The three of us are going away for the weekend to celebrate the wedding officially, but we have longer honeymoon plans for the summer. Will you stay with us next week when we come home again?"

Ash glanced at us again, her brilliant blue eyes troubled.

Then she looked back at Laura, nodding slowly. "Yeah, sure. I'd love to catch up with you. It's been too long."

I cleared my throat and held out my hand to Ashleigh. "Would you like a tour of the property?"

I may as well start the ball rolling. We had the weekend to woo her before Laura returned from her honeymoon, and I didn't want to waste a single moment. Ash glared with impressive attitude. If she'd been a mountain lion, her fur coat would have bristled. "No bloody way. And keep your hands to yourself."

She turned in a flurry of silver silk and beautiful brown hair. Her spine straightened as she stomped her way up the steps and into the house.

I had to admit I was already proud to call her ours.

Laura giggled, drawing our attention. "You two are going to have your hands full if she's yours."

"She's ours," we said in unison. My voice sounded deep and gravelly, even to my ears.

Scott's voice held more pain than I expected.

Before I could ask him what was going on, Brandon and Tyler strolled up and wrapped their hands around their new bride.

"Hey, Scott, Jack." Brandon's voice pushed into my head, and I forced my gaze away from the retreating form of our mate and back to the hosts.

I nodded mechanically at Brandon, but couldn't stop my attention from straying to the house again.

"Congratulations to you all," Scott said, as we began to edge away. "We, uh, have to..."

I couldn't speak for him, but I was pretty sure he didn't want our long-awaited fated mate getting too far away either.

Laura laughed at us. "Go, go. You have the weekend with her, then I'll be back and will have her from Monday."

I gave Laura a grateful smile and took off toward the house. Scott quickly followed.

"I can't believe she's really..." His voice drifted off, as if he couldn't say the actual words.

I grinned at him as we mounted the steps. Pausing on the well-made back patio, we peered through the door and inside the house. Ashleigh stood with our aunt Rosalie in the open plan kitchen.

"She really is our mate, Scott. Can you believe it? I mean, fucking twenty-five years and we..." I trailed off, a lump rising in my throat. "We finally found her."

Scott and I had decided when we were young that the prophecy we'd been told about perfect pairs was bullshit. We'd gone our separate ways, followed our gonads and married women who didn't suit us.

Then, even worse, we'd bred with the bitches who'd tormented us for twenty years. Two divorces and five children between us.

Scott cleared his throat with a rough cough. "I...I didn't think she was real."

I nodded and couldn't help the hopeful smile that spread across my face. My heart was pounding and my hands were shaking. A thin film of sweat covered my brow. "I feel alive, Scott. For the first time in...forever."

Scott nodded and wiped his own brow with a handkerchief. I laughed, something inside my chest opening like a bird spreading its wings.

I jerked my head toward the kitchen. "Let's go."

"Wait." Scott grabbed my arm, stopping me from going to our woman.

I twisted my arms out of his grip and glared at him. "What's wrong now?"

"Do you think, uh, we should talk to her one at a time?" He hesitated. "You know... since she's not a shifter. She won't understand about perfect pairs."

I frowned and glanced through the glass patio door. Aunt Rosalie was still engrossed in conversation with Ashleigh.

"That's probably a good idea." I stared at him, clenching my teeth and putting some heat into the glare. I was the oldest and yet he'd been the one to touch her first. "I'll go in, and we can tag team if need be."

Scott's jaw pulled tight and he huffed through his nostrils, but after a moment he nodded. "Okay, but don't take all night. I want to speak to her too."

I chuckled and turned around, squaring my shoulders as I stared at our woman.

Let the chase begin.

CHAPTER

TWO

ASHLEIGH

I stood with Rosalie in the kitchen and struggled to focus on the woman in front of me. Her face lit up every time I asked a question about her children so I kept that conversation going while my mind reeled with what had just occurred outside.

What on earth had happened when Jack and Scott touched me? It was like they'd reached inside me and attached electrodes to my soul, shooting pleasure into my belly and destroying any ability I had of holding my own body weight upright.

If Jack hadn't stepped forward when he had, I would probably have ended up on the ground, a pulsing mess of sensations.

I was a thirty-five-year-old divorcee with a successful business and multiple degrees. It was ridiculous to have so little control, all of a sudden.

I could sense the two men standing outside the door watching me. I was trying—God knew I was *trying*—to forget their presence, but if my gaze had been capable of dividing in two, one part would be staring straight at those men, warning them to back off.

Why were they showing so much interest in me?

They were gorgeous, maybe ten years or so my senior, and sexy as hell. Men like that were never interested in *me*.

"It must have been hard taking time away from your business to come down for the wedding," Rosalie said. "Or do you have someone you trust back home to run everything for you?"

Yet again, I forced my brain back to the conversation with Laura's new mother-in-law, Rosalie.

There was only one way to do that properly, so I fully turned my back on the men standing on the patio. "Um, a week isn't too much time to take off, luckily. But yes, any longer and it becomes more stressful. I have some fantastic pharmacists working for me, and I trust them not to burn the place down while I'm gone."

"That sounds interesting," a man said from behind me. "Who's burning what down?"

I jumped, knowing it was one of the two before turning around. My heart pounded against my ribs and heat spread up into my cheeks as Jack sauntered through the patio door.

He strolled over and kissed me on the cheek. I gulped air into my lungs at the desire to turn so he could plant one on my actual mouth.

He smiled at Rosalie. "Hey, Aunt Rosalie. Congratulations on finally getting those two married off."

"Yeah, well, they had to wait for the right woman to come along, didn't they, Jack?"

Rosalie's stern tone snapped my attention back to the conversation.

A slash of red colored Jack's handsome cheeks. "Yes, they were much smarter than I was."

What did that mean? He wasn't wearing a ring, although that wasn't always the case for men. Was he married? Or divorced? Had he let someone go?

Rosalie turned to me, blue eyes glowing with warmth. "Jack, have you met Laura's cousin Ashleigh? She's a pharmacist from Toronto."

My belly tightened as Jack's sparkling azure eyes met mine, a smile tilting up his full lips. "I did, outside, though I didn't realize she was a pharmacist. We only spoke briefly."

I swallowed the lump that rose in my throat and straightened my shoulders. I could do this. I could conduct a conversation with a man I couldn't keep my eyes off. "What do you do, Jack?"

That smile widened, lighting a path into the pit of my belly, pulling on an area between my thighs that I'd believed died a long time ago. After my ex-husband had done such a good job of destroying my self-esteem, I hadn't thought a man would ever appeal to me again.

I squeezed my thighs together and almost gasped at the jolt of longing. I'd never believed in lust at first sight, but this had to be it.

"I'm a football coach for the local high school," Jack said. "I played pro ball for a few years after college."

My blood cooled like the heat had never been there. He answered with such arrogance, as though playing football was actually impressive. I looked away. What was the easiest way of escaping? Maybe say I needed the bathroom?

"Oh, that's nice. Would you excuse me?" I turned away. "Rosalie, could you tell me where the bathroom is, please?"

Jack's eyes widened and his mouth fell open slightly.

Yeah, I'm not impressed by the fact that you can kick a bloody ball around, buddy.

I smiled at Rosalie and tried to ignore the odd pain in my gut. It was as though my body wanted me to stay. But why would I want to talk to a footballer, for God's sake? Thick as a brick and more focused on his body than anything of importance.

Rosalie sucked in a breath, as though she were shocked by my rude reaction to Jack, but I could barely breathe. I *had* to get away. How stupid did they think I was to fall for the charm of a philanderer? Which he no doubt was.

Rosalie pointed behind me. "Head down the hallway and it's the third door on the left."

I gave Jack a half-smile and bobbed my head. "Nice to meet you, again."

I turned on my heel and headed in the direction Rosalie had sent me, my blood hot in my veins.

I tried to focus on the house around me, to help calm down. It really was incredible. The ceilings were high and the rooms spacious, yet the whole place had that cozy home feeling that only special people managed.

I stopped outside the bathroom and stared at the framed picture on the wall. It was of Tyler and Brandon, about fifteen years earlier. They were all arm and legs. Their noses were too big for their faces, but their smiles were exactly the same—cheeky and oh-so-charming.

My cousin was a lucky woman, indeed. Assuming of course Brandon and Tyler didn't turn into the arrogant pigs most men had proven themselves to be, in my world.

Judging by the strength of their mother, they'd be skinned alive if they even tried.

"I love that photo." Rosalie had snuck up behind me and poked her nose over my shoulder.

I turned and smiled at her. "My cousin seems very happy, Rosalie. I'm so glad she's found someone...um...*two* someones."

Laura was sort of married to both of them. At least, I thought so. I'd read the invitation wrong and turned up two hours early. Once I realized my error I'd expected to find a back yard set up for a wedding, but with not a guest in sight. I'd decided to just sit down and relax for a while. God knows, I needed the rest.

Instead, I'd been shocked to walk in and find that the wedding was in full swing. And not only that. At the custom made altar stood my cousin with *two* grooms, instead of one.

My shock hadn't lasted, though. Laura's happiness had been too evident, and it was impossible to judge her harshly.

"*Men* who will look after her. Love her," I added.

Rosalie swivelled so she was blocking my escape into the bathroom, her abundant figure beautiful in its feminine shape. "She is lucky, but so are they."

I nodded. "I don't know your sons at all, but I do know Laura. That woman is a gem."

Rosalie crossed her arms over her impressive bust and looked at me with intense eyes.

I cocked my head. "Is there something you want to tell me, Rosalie?"

Her beautiful eyes were troubled as she worried her lower lip with her teeth. "My sons are a perfect pair, which means they are perfect complements to each other, in both looks and personality. Pretty much think of it as a perfect man, divided into two."

I laughed, the bubble spreading through my belly and up. I had to cover my mouth with my hand before the laugh became too loud. "Well, in my experience, that would be the only way to get a halfway decent man."

Rosalie frowned and I stopped laughing. That was probably too much information for a woman I barely knew.

She continued. "Jack and Scott are a perfect pair too, so please don't dismiss Jack because you think he isn't educated enough. He has a college degree, but chooses to spend his life educating young men about the strength of their bodies. Scott is a scientist with the government. He chose a different path to his brother."

Heat seared a path up my neck and blossomed across my face as shame swamped me. The tone she had taken with me could only be called *chastising*, and I felt it right down to my sickened belly.

Guilty as charged.

"I don't like football, or footballers, Rosalie," I said. "I've recently endured a nasty divorce, so please excuse my rude behavior. I'm not interested in anyone, especially two men who..."

I trailed off, my cross-referencing brain pulling together fibers of information that I'd gathered from the afternoon.

Two men? Oh, my God!

I took a breath and stared directly into Rosalie's face, seeing the truth there before I even asked the dreaded question. "Rosalie, do all perfect pairs marry one woman?"

I placed my hands on my hips and barely stopped myself from tapping my foot when she looked down.

Then she looked back up, her mouth tight as she nodded. "Yes. They are designed to find one woman who is perfect for them."

They... what? Did she mean in their family, their culture?

Hang on! They better not think that's me!

"Is that why Jack and Scott are pursuing me?" I asked. "Does it have something to do with that weird electricity thing?"

Rosalie's gaze sharpened and she stepped a little closer. "Electricity thing?"

I frowned and rubbed my hands together, remembering the first contact I'd had with Scott, and then Jack when his arms had wrapped around me.

Those moments of pure sensation. Neither science nor common sense could explain why I'd had such a strong reaction to two men I'd never met before. Perhaps Rosalie had some answers.

"Yes," I began slowly. "When they touched me, something happened. It felt like sparks flying through my skin, lighting up my blood."

Rosalie's eyes widened and her breathing sped up.

Why was she getting excited?

"And my nephews?" she asked, a strange note in her voice. "How did they react?"

Not as weirdly as I did, which was embarrassing.

I shrugged. "Not sure, but they haven't stopped staring at me. I feel like I'm being pursued, which is ridiculous, I know. I sound vain, which isn't me at all, but—"

A strange giggle burst out of Rosalie, which she stifled with her hand. "Sorry. Okay, well, thank you. I'll leave you alone and well...yeah."

She disappeared in a hurry.

What had that been about? I didn't even try to guess. Instead, I stepped into the bathroom with no real need to use it, and simply sat on the toilet with the lid down. I needed space to catch my breath for a few minutes.

I'd taken a week of leave to attend my cousin's wedding, but I had another reason, too. I needed time-out to recover from the past year, which had been nothing short of hell.

Now this.

What sort of rabbit hole had I fallen into?

Scott

I SWAGGERED into the kitchen and faced my barely-older brother.

I was still in shock over the idea that we may have found our fated mate, but the jury was still out on whether we could make it work. For me, too much water had passed under the bridge in this lifetime to ever be happy again.

I crossed my arms, staring at Jack.

How had the golden boy fared with a woman who could supposedly handle us both, if Fate were to be believed?

Not that I've ever met a woman who could do that.

"Go well, did it?"

A low growl left Jack's throat as he glared at me, his blue eyes firing like a roiling lightning storm. I couldn't help the grin that spread across my face. Struck out, had he?

"What? You're the suave one," I said. "Whatcha do wrong?"

Jack was way more charming and handsome than me. He was also the one who had always believed that our fated mate was still out there. Even with all the evidence to the contrary.

It was hilarious that he'd struck out so quickly.

"I'm an ex-footballer," he said, with a roll of his eyes. "That seems to be a problem."

My eyebrows shot up. Since when did my twin being an amazing sportsman, with all the successes and muscular body that went with it, cause a problem?

"You're kidding me," I said. "I've never met a woman who didn't love the fact that you played football."

He shrugged, his posture tight and stiff through his shoulders. "She's pretty smart, I think. Probably believes I'm a typical jock. We both know some footballers can be a bit thick."

My interest piqued like a cat popping its head up from a sleeping position. "Smart? Like how?"

Laura was a vet, so maybe her cousin was, too? Not that I had an easy time believing that one woman was made for both of us, but if she were, I'd need her to be smart. Not to mention a great communicator, affectionate, loving, and sensual as hell...

Yeah, good fucking luck. You've looked forever and never found a woman who came within streets of that.

Jack shrugged. "She's a pharmacist. I think. She owns her own business."

I inhaled sharply and moved my weight from foot to foot.

My heart thumped louder inside my chest as I took in that important piece of information. That meant she was more than smart.

She was *highly intelligent* and probably had a decent amount of common sense, too, if she ran a business. "Wow, well, she's got brains, then."

"Yeah, and the booty..." Jack whistled and pulled a face that was close to a grimace.

I lifted a brow, surprised that Jack thought Ashleigh had a good physique. "I thought you liked 'em lean?"

I didn't mind lots of curves, but Jack always seemed to go for the women whose waist could be spanned with two hands. Two of Jack's ex-girlfriends would need to be stuck together, to make up the weight of Ashleigh's voluptuous figure.

Jack shrugged, thrusting his hands into his pockets. "They're just the ones that hang around the places I go. The gym, football games. I don't pick them on purpose. Besides, her curves are a fucking turn-on."

Aunt Rosalie came at us from down the hall, bustling like a steam train, her face set and determined. "I can't believe it! She's your mate, isn't she? After all this time, you've found her!"

I groaned and threw my head back.

The whole family knew how I felt about this! Even if there was such a woman for us, it was too bloody late to have any sort of life with her.

I growled at the ceiling. "How can you say that to us, Aunt Rosalie?"

I brought my head back down and glared. She just beamed back, her blue eyes bright and clear.

Fuck!

"Because you two are following her around like puppies and you had the instant contact fire bolt, didn't you?" She slapped her hand against my arm. "And what do you mean? I know you both stupidly married women who didn't suit you, but that doesn't mean that you don't still have the perfect woman out there waiting for you."

She leaned closer, her gaze flicking between the two of us. "And it sounds like you're going to have your work cut out for you. Ashleigh has just gone through a messy divorce and is pretty cut up. You're going to have to work a little bit of magic."

Stop! I don't want to know anything about her.

I turned and walked back through the glass doors and stood on the patio, my heart galloping in my chest as though it were trying to escape.

I didn't want this. I *didn't!*

Sure, I'd wanted to touch her to see what would happen, but I hadn't thought I'd actually *feel* anything when I did.

I thought touching her would prove the strange feelings flowing through me were wrong, but it had done the opposite.

Jack came up beside me. His big hand slapped me on the back and the breath left my lungs in a fast, painful rush.

Damn caveman.

"You okay, bro?" he asked.

I shook my head and crossed my arms over my chest, then dropped them when the move pulled on my shirt too much and made it feel like a boa constrictor was wrapping around my torso and arms. Bloody monkey suits.

I preferred casual attire, any day. I even got to wear a t-shirt and loose lab coat at work.

"Fine," I said with an edge.

Jack chuckled and I sighed, some of the fight going out of me.

This was Jack. My best mate, my brother. He had been there for every moment of my life. All the good and most of the bad.

No one knew more about how much damage my ex-wife had done to me. "I don't want to get married again, Jack."

There was that chuckle again.

"That's cool," he said, "but I'm going for it. You don't mind, I assume?"

A heavy growl rose and vibrated through my chest. My hands balled into fists and the mountain lion within me rose to the surface.

No! She's mine too!

"Settle down, Scott, it's okay." Jack's placating tone and hand on my arm was enough to calm the lion.

I was so used to controlling him that he submitted quickly. Twenty years with an abusive, degrading human wife tested one's control to its limit.

"I don't..." Eloquent words weren't possible at the moment. My chest tightened further, a sense of helplessness washing over me. "Oh, fuck it. I can't do this, Jack. I'm going home. Tell the boys and Laura I said good-bye."

I gave Jack a smile that was closer to a grimace. I couldn't do any better right now. Crow's feet lined his normally young-looking face as he studied me.

He was worried about me.

I slapped my hand on his shoulder. "Don't stress, big brother. All good."

I stepped through the crowd of family and picked up my jacket. Thankfully, I'd brought my own car, and the kids were with my ex for the weekend.

No one stopped me as I made my way through Rosalie and John's house. I flinched as I stepped through the carved front door. I took a few steps down the path, and then realized I couldn't resist the tug of the front door's beauty. I had to look once more. I turned and clenched my jaw against the feelings that assailed me.

It was only a door. A pretty entranceway to a house.

It's more than that... and you know it.

I sighed and let my shoulders sag, the deep ache and longing flowing over me like a cold shower. Within the door was the carved shape of a mountain lion, which was beautiful on its own, but the image was also designed to be deceptive.

In the backdrop were four other lions carved into the wood. The family surrounding and supporting their alpha, their father, their husband. I'd wanted that. I still did. The wooden carving stared at me, mocking me with everything Rosalie and John had together.

Everything I didn't.

I blinked back tears and made my way through the throng of cars until I found my old Mercedes, jumped in, and started the car.

I'd been young and blind when I'd married my wife. I hadn't believed any of the stories about perfect pairs and I'd hoped to be happy. Hoped that the woman I bred with, trusted, and loved, would be right for me.

But I'd never been more wrong, and I'd paid for it. Time and time again.

Why would anything be any different now? Ashleigh was a woman, like all others. Surely, she couldn't be that unique?

I tightened my grip on the wheel and put my foot on the accelerator. I couldn't afford to make any more mistakes. My heart wouldn't recover from another break. I'd barely survived the first time.

No. The best thing to do was run, hard and fast. And never look back.

THREE

I sat on a chair facing the dance floor they'd erected in John and Rosalie's back yard. I took a sip of my beer and let the cold hops slide down my gullet, contentment settling over me in a way it had never had.

We'd found our mate. Our true mate. And my life was officially *made.*

My eyes trained on the sway of Ashleigh's rounded hips while she danced with Laura on the makeshift wooden stage. She was one hell of a sensual woman.

"She's a beautiful woman, Jack," Uncle John said as he stepped up beside me, laying a hand on my arm. His touch was both reassuring and paternal.

"Yeah, she is. Thanks, Uncle John."

I continued to watch Ashleigh dance to the music, her lush ass and breasts moving and swinging in an enticing way. She threw back her head and laughed at something Laura said, color flowing into her cheeks and brightening up her whole face.

Something bad had happened to her, I was sure. Rosalie and Laura had both alluded to it, but I didn't know what it was. A messy divorce was one thing—I'd had one of those—but there was something more going on and I was determined to get to the bottom of it.

"You spoke to her much yet?" John asked.

I chuckled and shook my head. "Yeah, for all of two minutes. She found out I was just a football jock and bolted."

John's eyes widened as his mouth fell open. "You're kidding me?"

I burst into laughter, drawing the attention of the people in the area, including Ashleigh, who quickly turned away again with a slight tilt of her chin. "Nope, I'm afraid not. Miss Pharmacist thinks I'm not suitable."

John frowned. "Does she know anything about perfect pairs?"

You mean the fact that Scott will make up for all my shortcomings?

I shrugged and took another sip of beer, loving the fresh taste down my throat.

I smiled at my uncle. "Not unless Aunt Rosalie or someone else explained it to her. If she had, she wouldn't have been worried about me being a footballer. Scott's smart enough for both of us. He's always been strong where I'm weak."

John huffed. "Yeah, and if you ask Scott, you make up for everything he lacks. You each have your strengths. It's not about weaknesses."

I shrugged, not particularly caring about semantics at the moment. All I wanted to know was when and how I could get into Ashleigh's pants.

My body was aching in the weirdest way. Like I needed a run. My system was jumpy and tight, yet I'd worked out this morning pretty hard. Amazingly, it seemed that exercise wasn't the solution to my current predicament.

I needed sex.

Preferably long, hard, and all-consuming. Not that I'd had decent sex in a long time, but there were always women around if I really needed them.

Yeah, right. Like you'll touch another woman now that you've met Ash.

"Jack! I didn't realize you were here." Tania stepped up in front of me, stopping and smiling as though she hadn't been stalking me all night.

Speak of the devil, here's one of those available women now...

John got up out of his chair and nodded toward me. "I think I'll take my leave, Jack."

"Yeah, no worries, Uncle John." I gave him a wink and he shook his head with a chuckle and walked away.

Tania wasn't sitting down, and I felt in a less powerful position being lower than her, so I stood up with a groan. "Hello Tania, how are you?"

She went up on her tiptoes and kissed me on the lips, lingering a little too long for just a hello. I pulled back, a chill snaking up my spine.

I swung my gaze around to find Ash glaring at me with a half-open mouth, before she disappeared back into the circle of dancers.

I grinned, happiness filling me up over her obvious display of jealousy. I turned back to Tania, who cooed and made slutty eyes at me.

"I'm good, Jack, but you never called me back for a second date. Naughty, naughty." She smacked me lightly on the hand, and I bit back the warning growl that rose in my throat.

She didn't know it yet—no one did—but I was officially off the market. *Forever.*

"No, darlin', I didn't, and I can't now," I said. "Can you let all the women know that Scott and I have found our mate?"

I broke the news with a smile, but it didn't stop her expression from clouding, her eyes spitting fire at me. Bloody shifter women and their fiery tempers.

"You're fucking kidding me! Since when?"

I grinned and couldn't stop reaching out and giving her a little tap under the chin. She really was ugly when she let her true personality come out.

"Nope, I'm not," I said. "Does it matter when? Just spread the word for us, okay?"

Tania hissed through her teeth, and I stared her down. Part of me couldn't believe I'd taken her into my bed on one occasion.

One time too many.

I'd rarely met a more selfish female. My mind shifted to Ashleigh and the change she would make to our life. My belly fluttered with excitement. I would never have to date another woman again.

Thank God for that!

I laughed as Tania flung her hair over her shoulder and sauntered away. I never thought I'd be happy to see the end of my single life, but I was.

Deliriously so.

If Tyler and Brandon's obvious contentment was anything to go by, then my brother's and my future was looking a hell of a lot brighter.

Brandon suddenly tapped me on the shoulder. "Looks like she's leaving."

My gaze snapped to the dance floor where Ash was picking up a coat and kissing Laura goodbye.

"Thanks for the heads-up, cousin."

I jumped off the patio and headed over to where my woman stood, enjoying the nervous tightening in my belly as I approached her.

Ash pulled out her cell phone from a small hand bag and tapped at the screen a few times.

"You need a ride?" I asked as I stopped in front of her.

She looked up, her eyes clouded by alcohol, then there was a flick of her eyebrows that showed her registering who I was.

You're aware of me too, aren't you, beautiful?

"No, I'm calling a cab, thank you," she said.

Laura stepped up beside me, squeezing my arm. "Ash, you won't get a cab out this far. There's barely any in town. Let Jack take you home. He's safe as pie, I promise. I'll vouch for him."

Well, I wouldn't have said that myself, but I appreciated Laura's support.

"Where are you staying? The Trenthy Inn?" I asked. It was the only decent accommodation this side of the city, and I wouldn't want her staying anywhere else.

Ash nodded, glancing between Laura and me like an animal pressed into a corner.

"Thanks, Jack." Laura patted me on the shoulder like it was all sorted and headed back to the party.

Ash sighed, her shoulders sagging in defeat as she placed her cell phone back in her bag and pulled on a black jacket that had been slung over the back of a nearby chair. "Shouldn't you be taking someone else home?"

I shook my head, placing my hand on the small of her back, and guided her around the house and toward my car. "No, my brother went home hours ago."

"I was talking about the redhead."

The words were said with so much spite I couldn't help the chuckle that escaped my lips. "Jealous, beautiful? You don't need to be. I told her to take a hike."

Ash's eyes flicked up at me before she pulled the jacket tighter around her body.

Not many people liked how honest I could be, but I didn't want to be anything else.

"This is mine." I indicated the silver four-wheel drive, and Ash moved around to the passenger side.

I clicked the button so that the doors unlocked and Ash slid in and buckled her seat belt. I shook my head and moved to my own door.

She was such an independent little thing.

I climbed in and started the car, carefully negotiating down the road still full of vehicles. The party would go well into the night, probably only stopping when the sun peeked over the mountains.

I turned on the radio and began to hum, not wanting to rush her into a conversation she wasn't ready for. Trenthy was a good twenty minutes away. We had time.

Ashleigh stared out the window, not speaking. After a few minutes, she turned back to me with a jerk and a huff. "Why didn't you go home with the redhead? She obviously wanted you."

Good reading of the play.

I glanced over at her and grinned before I returned my gaze to the road. "Honestly? Because I'm done with dating. I told her that Scott and I were no longer single and that she needed to tell the rest of the women."

"The other women? Why would she need to do that?"

I shrugged, not quite sure she wanted all the details about our shifter family yet.

"We have a pretty tight-knit community," I said. "Word will spread quickly now."

Ash crossed her arms over her chest and went back to staring out the window.

Butterflies fluttered like crazy in my belly. I held my breath and waited for her to ask the more obvious question.

Go on, beautiful. I know you wanna ask.

Her words lacked heat when they finally filled the quiet of the truck's cabin. "Why are you both now off the market?"

I glanced over to find her still staring out the window. I couldn't read her expression. Why not tell her? She'd obviously seen the ceremony today, and someone must have told her about us.

"Because we've met our perfect mate," I said. "After twenty long years of searching, it's about time, really."

The Trenthy Inn was up ahead and I slowed down to park on the opposite side of the street. I turned the engine off and unclipped my seat belt, watching as she did the same.

"You don't mean..." She finally lifted her head and stared at me, her blue eyes wide and as deep as an ocean. Like I could dive straight in.

"I do." I reached over and cupped her face, pulling her toward me when she didn't resist. I moved to meet her halfway.

Our lips met and I gasped as spiralling pleasure consumed me. I pulled her closer, sliding my tongue between her open lips and tasting her for the first time.

Oh, wow!

I shuddered where I sat, my body filling up with an ecstasy I'd never experienced before, confirming without a doubt that she was the one. Her sweet mouth was addictive and my heart stuttered in my chest when she moaned and pulled away, looking up with eyes full of lust. And also laced with fear.

~

Ashleigh

Tingles of heat swamped my senses, running down my arms and legs and playing havoc with my hormones.

I needed this man on a carnal level I'd never experienced before. Never even *felt* this within me before. My core was aching and tight, desperate with need.

"What...Why?" I couldn't put a full sentence together as I stared at the gorgeous man who'd just kissed me.

Memories of my marriage came flooding back. The pain. The humiliation.

I straightened up and ignored the pleasure coiling in my belly.

Not again, no. I'd promised myself, never again.

But it never felt like *this*, a traitorous voice said in my head.

"Thanks for the ride, Jack."

I grabbed my bag and opened the door, my knees shaking as I forced myself to step out of the vehicle and begin the trek to my room.

Oh, God, my legs are so heavy I can barely walk!

The huge car helped me to stay upright as I clung to the hood and pulled myself around the SUV. Just a hundred feet across the street, and I'd be inside my room.

I just had to get the key out of my bag…

Jack stepped out of the car.

"What's your story, little spitfire?" he asked as he came around to my side of the car and wrapped his arm around my waist, supporting me.

His touch felt just right, and as much as my head told me to wiggle out of the embrace, my body didn't obey.

Together, we made our way across the road and up the stairs to my room.

His strength and warmth drew me in. I couldn't resist pressing against his body, my need to be close to him almost as startling as the instant lust that had flared between us.

"My story?" I repeated.

"Yeah, your story."

He lifted me up the last step, then eased me down. As his heat left my skin, my stomach contracted. Then a shiver ran over me as though I'd stepped out of a hot shower and into a cold room.

A whimper escaped my throat before I clenched my teeth together.

He grinned and stayed close as I opened the door to my room. Should I ask him in?

No. It was too soon for that, but amazingly, I was tempted.

If his kisses were anything to go by, then this man would be an amazing lover.

I turned to look at him and he tapped his chest with his finger as he started to speak. "I got married twenty years ago to a selfish woman. I thought she wanted me for me… but soon found out it was just the football fame and money side of things she was interested in."

My mouth fell open. The man in front of me, despite my initial reservations, was obviously lovely—and bloody gorgeous. What kind of woman would only want him for his money?

"You're kidding me?" I said, hanging on the door, one foot over the threshold.

He shook his head, his eyes serious as he continued to stare at me.

"We have two teenage sons who live with their mom in the city," he said. "I talk to them every couple of days and they come visit every few weeks. My ex and I are pretty civil these days, but she was never the right person for me."

All the strength in me drained away. This man was so honest and blunt, not to mention totally fucking hot. How was I going to withstand his advances if he chose to pursue me?

Maybe a little of my own history would put him off?

"I was married for five years to a guy with small-man syndrome," I said.

Jack flinched. "Ouch."

I shrugged, trying my best not to grimace as feelings of inadequacy flowed over me. "As I became more successful with work, he became more controlling, more emotionally abusive. In the end, I practically ran away and can't imagine ever trusting a man again."

I eyed him, needing to get my point across. I wasn't good enough for these men.

Jack just stared at me, being totally unreadable.

I sighed. "Jack, you and Scott are obviously great guys, but you're wrong if you think I'm this perfect mate," I said. "As my ex-husband would tell you, I'm fat, lazy, bad in bed, and selfish. You don't really want me. No one does."

Jack barked out a laugh, and then coughed to cover it as I glared at him.

How could he laugh when I'd just admitted all my faults to him? Did he really think I was joking?

He stepped up and slipped his hands around my waist, gripping my large ass and pulling me into the cradle of his pelvis.

"Sweetheart, you are beautiful, and fiery, and everything about you is a fucking huge turn-on," he said in a low husky voice. "If your abusive idiot ex convinced you that you weren't enough woman for him, then that's his problem. You are more than enough for me and my brother."

And that was the other thing! I wasn't being shared between two men!

I cleared my throat. "Yeah, about that. You can't honestly think I'll just fall into bed with you guys? Both of you?"

Jack's mouth descended, effectively shutting off all communication between my brain and my ability to speak.

His kisses were magic. My arms encircled his neck to hold him close, and all thoughts vanished like they'd never been. I moaned and my eyes slid shut.

I couldn't help it. I let myself be carried away in a maelstrom of sensation.

When he finally lifted his head, I couldn't remember what I'd meant to say.

He grinned down at me. "How 'bout I pick you up tomorrow and take you out for lunch? I can tell you more about my brother then."

He kissed me gently on the nose, turned, and bounded partway down the stairs while I fell back against the door, my knees weak as water. "What about Scott?"

Jack grinned and waved. "Get inside so I know you're safe, and I'll see you at noon tomorrow."

I sighed and nodded, giving in to my body's need to lie down. I shut the door, staggered across the room, and collapsed onto the soft bed.

So, Scott had some secrets, did he? I sighed and ran my hands over my full breasts and ample thighs. How did Jack make me feel so sexy and desirable?

I'd *never* felt that way before.

I undressed quickly and slid beneath the covers. It was such a luxury to be in a bed that was automatically made for me every day, and with sheets I didn't have to wash.

My ex wouldn't allow me to hire any help for our home. He said it was because he didn't want any strangers in our house, but he'd let slip once it was because he wanted me to feel overrun and stressed all the time.

Made him feel good about himself.

The simple truth was, my business made enough money for me to pay for a cleaner, an ironing lady, and a chef if I really wanted one. But I'd been putting it off, assuming that my ex was right—and that I could do everything on my own. And therefore, should.

But it was time I stopped the ghosts of my past determining my future.

That was the first thing I was going to do when I got home. Hire a housekeeper.

I pulled the cover up over my head and groaned as my situation played around inside my head. Despite my reservations, something kept pulling me back to Jack and everything he encompassed.

'Jinxed Ash' and two hot men... What could go wrong?

FOUR

JACK

I pulled up outside the café, my woman already in the car beside me. "Ready, beautiful?"

Ash frowned but nodded.

For an intelligent, once-married woman, she sure was a skittish thing.

I undid my seat belt and jumped from the car. I rounded the trunk, stepping up to her side, and opened the door. "What's wrong?" I asked.

"Nothing," she said, taking my hand and letting me help her out.

Yeah, right.

"You frowned when I said, *ready, beautiful?*"

She looked away as color slashed across her rounded cheeks. "I'm not beautiful, Jack. I know that. And I've never handled compliments well, especially when they're not true."

Oh, God, that bastard really did a number on you, didn't he, sweetheart?

"Really, well..." I pulled her around so that she was facing me, holding her tight against my body and sliding my hands into the back pockets of her jeans.

I gently thrust my groin in an obvious way and looked directly into her eyes. I wanted her to know that she was desired.

I leaned forward and whispered in her ear. "Ash, you have a beautiful face, the hottest ass I've ever seen in denim, and I cannot wait to get you naked and see what the rest of you looks like."

She slapped at my chest and tried to pull away, but the reluctant smile on her full lips told me that she didn't mind the way I had just talked to her.

"Come on," I said. "Let's get something to eat before I drag you back to my bedroom so I can feast on you."

I grabbed hold of her hand and she gripped my fingers tight, her breath hitching as though she were nervous when I led her into the café.

"Booth for two," I said to the waitress, who directed us to a corner that was perfect for secret touches. When she sat down, I slid in right next to her, and ordered the special for both of us without glancing at the rest of the menu. As soon as the waitress had left, I grinned at Ash. I had her all to myself again.

"I almost don't want to bring Scott into this," I said. "I'm having too much fun with you myself."

I slid across the leather booth until we were hip to hip, and I could run my hand over her thigh and grip the denim above her knee.

She muffled a squeal and pushed my hand down closer to her knee.

Damn, my hormones were high. Adrenaline slid through my bloodstream like red-hot lava, my muscles bulking and stretching. The coiling tension centered deep in my belly made my cock ache.

Gratitude flowed through me as I said a silent prayer of thanks.

Over the past five years, my sex drive had waned. I got bored easily and the women I dated didn't touch my heart in any way.

It was exhausting to make myself bed women so I could get enough physical touch and intimacy to survive. But for Ashleigh, my body felt like it had turned back into its twenty-year-old self. All raging hormones and energy.

I'd trained this morning at the gym and had been able to lift more than I had in a decade. I had a spring in my step, too. There was something to look forward to for the first time in years.

Ash folded a napkin, then fidgeted with the salt and pepper shakers. "Why do you have to bring Scott into anything? Are you going to explain more about this perfect pair thing?"

A fluttering of pride sprang to life inside my chest. I'd never dated a woman with intelligence before. I'd been happy enough if they could manage a little bit of common sense. But Ashleigh was smart, very smart. She'd keep me and Scott on our toes.

"So someone did tell you about us?"

She nodded, glancing toward the waitress who approached with our drinks. She placed them in front of us and then headed over to the next table.

"Rosalie told me about the family trait," Ash said. "The fraternal twin thing. You and Scott are a perfect pair like Brandon and Tyler, right?"

I grunted and took a sip of my Coke. "We are. But we stupidly ignored all the legends that told us to wait for our perfect mate, and we married the wrong women for us. We've been paying for it ever since."

With a frown, Ashleigh pulled her milkshake forward and took a long drink through the pink straw. "What do you mean by that?"

I sighed, dread sinking into my heart. It seemed too early to be airing dirty laundry. It could cause a rift, or worse... give her an excuse to leave us.

I swallowed hard. "Promise to hear me out all the way to the end?"

She sucked harder on her straw, nodded, and looked at me with her big blue eyes. I groaned and shifted in my chair as blood flowed to my rapidly-thickening cock.

Would she look up at me like that when she sucked my cock? Would she even want to do that, after I'd finished explaining things?

I rubbed both hands over my face, trying to focus on the topic at hand.

"I can tell you more about my ex-wife later, but that story's pretty simple. We just couldn't live together despite giving it a good go. As I said, she wanted my money, not me, and that soon became clear. We tried for a while, but it was the right decision not to be together anymore."

I stopped and took another sip of my drink. "But my brother's the one I want to talk about." I took a deep breath. "Scott's ex isn't as reasonable as mine."

Ashleigh's head came up and shot him a disbelieving look. "You said your ex was a selfish woman."

I tilted my head, easing my neck muscles to release the tension. "She is. But Scott's ex, Kerry... she's so much worse."

Ashleigh returned to sucking on her milkshake and made gesturing motions with her hand to continue. Now that I'd started the conversation, I had to finish it.

"Kerry was, well—*is*—degrading, demanding, and self-centered. She got pregnant on the sly so Scott had to marry her, then set about taking him apart at every turn. I don't know half of it because he doesn't tell me everything, but he was a broken man when they finally divorced."

The waitress returned with our food—chicken wraps and fries—and I picked up a chip, munching on it in an attempt to fill the cold in my gut.

I didn't want to tell Ash everything, but Kerry was beyond abusive. Emotional, physical at times, even screwing up Scott's sex drive to the point that it took years for him to get back to dating.

Ashleigh picked up her wrap and began eating, chewing thoughtfully.

"So, he's a bit of a tortured hero, huh?" she said at length.

A tortured what?

I cocked my head and stared at the little smile playing across her lips. Did she actually like the idea of fixing my brother?

Then she laughed and my brows lifted. What a sound! Like music designed just for me, it filled my heart with pleasure.

"A tortured hero in a romance book is the main character who has all the qualities a hero should have," she said. "He's intelligent, sexy, has a great sense of humor. But he's been tortured and needs lots of love, affection, and sex to help him heal. He's every woman's dream, really."

She snapped her mouth shut and blushed, looking away like a child who'd been caught with her hand in the candy jar.

Didn't mean to say that much, Ash?

I grinned. "I'll take your word for it. I wouldn't know shit about book heroes."

Ash glanced back at me, her eyes huge. She was waiting for something but I couldn't figure it out.

"What?" I picked up my fork and kept eating. This woman sure was a puzzle.

"I, um, feel a bit stupid," she began. "I'm assuming things I shouldn't."

I shrugged. I doubted that. "You're pretty cluey, as smart as Scott probably... so I doubt you're wrong. Whatcha assuming?"

She picked at her food and chewed with a frown creasing her forehead. "I don't want to say it out loud."

I couldn't stop myself. I reached over and smoothed the frown lines with my thumb, and then cupped her beautiful face in my palm when she turned toward me like a flower to the sun. "Damn, you're gorgeous."

Her cheeks grew redder and she glanced away. "Please don't lie to me, Jack."

I laughed, loudly enough to draw attention. I didn't care. Let them look. I was on my first date with the woman designed just for me. I couldn't be happier.

"You're kidding me, right? I don't lie, Ash. When I say you're gorgeous, I'm understating."

I tilted her chin so that I could look directly at her and lowered my voice. "And if I could be kissing you while being balls deep inside you right now, I would be."

"Jack!" Her eyes grew wide and her tone was outraged, yet she certainly made no move to run away from me.

I shrugged and let the chuckle rumble within my chest, happiness filling me up like a never-ending fountain. A few women in the past had enjoyed me talking dirty to them, but the reactions I'd received were moderate.

I had the feeling Ashleigh would be different. I'd aim to dirty-talk her into orgasm while we were in bed, and what a pleasure *that* would be.

"So, what were we talking about, Ash?"

She stared at me for a moment, her expression softening and the frown smoothing out. I reached for my drink and took a sip.

"You actually want me, don't you?"

The cold soda spurted out of my mouth and sprayed across the table as I tried to cough and laugh at the same time. Luckily, I'd aimed away from our food.

I grabbed at the napkin and wiped my mouth and nose, glaring at her. Why'd she go and say such a silly thing? I looked ridiculous. "Of course, we do! What do you think this is all about?"

When she continued to stare at me, I sighed and forced myself to slow down.

"Sorry," I said, "I forget you haven't grown up within our family and you don't know much about how perfect pairs work."

She half-smiled and nodded, which I took to mean she wanted me to continue talking.

"Perfect pairs, as you've probably been told by Rosalie, are a set of nonidentical twin boys who are both exact opposites and complements to each other."

"No female perfect pairs exist?" Ash asked.

I'd wondered that myself when I'd been younger.

"No, not that we know of. But anyway... what it means for us is that we can offer our mate, when we find her, a combination of physical and personality attributes that don't usually exist in one single male. I'm pretty rough-and-ready, and Scott's quieter and more cerebral. I'm more likely to throw you onto the bed and kiss you, whereas Scott likes to talk about everything."

She gave me a strange look. "Have you shared women before?"

I shuddered. "No, not at all. That was our main objection to the legend—neither of us liked the idea of sharing one woman."

When her smile dropped and her gaze fell to her lap, I could have kicked myself.

I reached out and lifted her chin up with my fingers.

"That was, until we met you, our true mate. We are designed to love you, together, and I finally know why. You're an amazing woman, Ashleigh. I know you need more than I can give you, alone. Together, Scott and I will fulfil all your emotional and physical needs." I leaned forward and waggled my eyebrows at her. "And I, for one, can't wait to start."

A soft laugh left her as she looked up, shaking her head slowly. "How do you make me believe that so easily?"

She picked up her wrap and began to eat again, humming a little as she ate. Was that a rhetorical question?

Man, this woman really was a puzzle.

"Because I mean it," I said. "We've been waiting for you our whole lives."

Ash giggled and continued eating, speaking between bites. "Me? Are you sure? You know I'm fat and I'm lousy in the bedroom? I've heard nothing but negative comments for years, and yet you think you can wipe it all away with one touch and make me into someone I'm not?"

I sat back. This was the core issue. "Sweetheart, you are neither fat, nor bad in bed, and I'll prove it to you. We've always been told that our perfect mate will match us in every way. Do you know what that is for me?"

She shook her head, looking up with sparkling, beautiful blue eyes. "Tell me."

I searched my soul and brought up everything I'd ever craved in a woman. "I could say I want someone with a high sex drive, who makes me laugh and will stick around forever, but do you know what I really want? A woman who will, of her own volition, kiss me every day."

"Pardon?"

I shrugged. That about covered it. If a woman wanted to kiss me, then the other things would fall into place. "I like affection, and my ex wasn't affectionate at all. I want to wake up with you wrapped around me, feel your hands on me. Then I want you to kiss me when I go to work, kiss me over dinner. I need touch. Sex, as well, but affection is separate. More important. I could go without sex. I can't go without touch. You think you can handle that?"

A tear welled and flowed down her cheek and she let it drip onto her t-shirt unchecked. "What about the housework? Don't you want someone who cooks your meals and keeps the house clean?"

I laughed. "I have a cleaner, and I cook for myself. I'm a pretty simple man. I want someone who loves me, Ash, and who I can love in return. I need a woman with a heart, who accepts me for exactly who I am, and shares that love with me."

Fuck, you're saying way too much, buddy.

I clamped my mouth shut as she slid closer. I didn't want to force her into anything.

She looked down at the table, biting her lip and gradually drawing her gaze back up to mine. She inhaled deeply and lifted her hands to cup my face.

I closed my eyes, enjoying the warmth of her palms against my skin. My eyelids snapped open again as she drew me in for a kiss.

She hesitated just before our lips met, her blue eyes showing so much uncertainty I had to clamp down on my need to take over and reassure her with words and touches how much I wanted her.

Finally, she lifted her chin and our lips met, a mutual sigh rising.

I let her guide me, her tongue teasing the seam of my lips before sliding in. Her touch spread through my senses and I moaned, reaching for her and bringing her closer while tasting her soft lips and unique scent.

My inner mountain lion stood up and purred, preening with happiness.

We'd found her.

Ash pulled back, her pupils dilated. "I'm a workaholic, I'm too pedantic about how I like things, I…"

She bit her lip, and I kissed the tip of her nose. "I love the fact that you're intelligent and hardworking. Be as pedantic as you like, just try not to rip me apart when I don't fall into line."

If she wanted a lap dog, there'd be trouble. Surely, Fate wouldn't design a woman like that for me, though.

Ash shook her head. "No, I wouldn't. It's just my things."

I kissed her forehead, her nose, her now slightly swollen pink lips. "Fantastic. But you'll kiss me every day? Smile at me and make me feel accepted just as I am?"

She hiccupped out a laugh. "You make it sound so easy and yet… I don't even live here! I'm on holidays for one week. How are we meant to find out if we suit each other in such a short amount of time, let alone the question of what we'll do if we want to stay together?"

I waved my hands to dismiss such foolish talk. "Don't even use the word 'if' in that sentence. And don't worry about all that, sweetheart. We'll sort something out. Jobs are flexible, and homes can be bought and sold. You're the most important thing to me. I don't care about anything else."

She stared at me, her beautiful eyes swimming with tears again.

A cold wave slipped over my soul as I forced myself to face one of my biggest insecurities. "Can you deal with the fact that I'm just a footballer? I know you think I'm not bright enough for you, but that's where Scott kicks in. He's super smart."

Ash pressed her lips to my mouth and just held herself there, melting against me and pushing waves of acceptance toward me.

When she pulled back, her eyes were blazing with heat. "Maybe you can teach me a thing or two about football so I can appreciate the game more?"

You bloody magnificent woman!

I chuckled and slid off the seat, pulling her with me so that we stood next to the table. I took out my wallet and dropped some cash next to our plates, more than enough to cover the cost.

She frowned at the money. "Um, no. I'll—"

"No." I cut her off, knowing what she was about to say. "I insist on paying today. If it bothers your sense of independence, Ash, you can pick up the next one."

"You're confident there'll be a next time, then?" A little smile played about her lips. It warmed my heart.

"Of course." *A thousand next times with you, beautiful.* "So, where are we going? You wanna see my property? Go find Scott, perhaps?"

She shook her head and gave me a sultry look.

My stomach muscles clenched and my breath hitched in my throat as I waited for her to make the next move.

Finally, she said, "No. I think you should take me back to the motel. I need to know if there is any truth to what you've been saying to me, Jack, and that means I need you to *show* me."

Surprise and lust moved over my body in alternate waves, making my groin tighten with anticipation. I planted one more quick kiss on her succulent lips before grabbing her hand and linking our fingers.

I liked having at least one hand on her at all times.

"Sure, sweetheart," I said. "That sounds like the perfect plan to me."

We made our way to the car and were back at her motel within minutes. My mate wanted me, I could see it... hear it... smell it.

Now the only question was, should I wait for Scott to make up his mind about her? Or mate with Ashleigh myself?

FIVE

ASHLEIGH

I slipped my key into the lock of my hotel room door and inhaled shakily. My tummy was tight and jumpy. Usually, that would be a sign that this wasn't the right thing to do.

But this time I knew it was generated by nerves. Good nerves. Terrified but excited about what might be about to happen.

I smiled over my shoulder as I took one of the most reckless steps of my life. "Do you want to come in?"

Jack grinned and rocked back on his heels as he stood opposite me in the hallway. His smile was devilishly handsome and his eyes sparkled with mischief. "Of course, I do. You sure you want me to?"

Before I lost my nerve, I nodded, turning my back on him, and opened the door with hands that shook.

I stepped through and held back the door so Jack could walk in, his swagger exaggerated as he moved. Butterflies wiggled inside my belly, my palms hot and sweaty as I rubbed them against my pants.

Jack said he wanted me, and if I was being honest, I wanted him too.

For the first time in years, I *really* wanted to be with a man. To feel his body on top of mine, the raw strength of him consuming me. No one had inspired such need in me before. My insecurities regarding my body and the lack of depth of feelings toward me, inhibited my responses.

Jack's honesty and animal need seemed to wipe all that away.

Wow.

I couldn't stop staring at him now that I gave myself permission to enjoy the view.

He was simply *huge.* Broad shoulders tapered into a lean waist and an ass so fine I was dying to dig my nails into it. He prowled into the room, radiating a sexual beat loud enough to drown out a rock concert.

When he looked at me, his blue eyes burned, and an answering heat welled up in my own blood.

He opened his arms wide. "You gonna come here, my beautiful woman?"

His words sank into me, slipping beneath the guard I held around my heart and penetrating deep. I'd invited him to my room, yet he was still giving me a free choice.

This wasn't going to be any uncomfortable, forced groping, laced with insecurity. Not with this man.

"I'm not yours yet, Jack," I teased as I walked forward, unable to resist the pull of such a magnetic man.

He was gorgeous in the traditional sense of the word, but my inability to resist him was built on so much more than his looks.

"Why do I feel so safe with you?" I asked as I moved closer.

I gasped as his big hands grabbed my ass and pulled me against him.

He squeezed my rump again and grinned, his face lighting up with that cheeky, happy smile that I was beginning to associate as being truly 'him'.

It filled me with elation.

"Because you *are* mine," he said. "You're our fated mate. This was planned long before we even existed. That's what our ancestors believe, anyway."

His lips pressed against mine but I pulled back so I could look at him. I slipped my arms around his solid neck. He smelled so good, like hazelnuts and man. I stroked the hair at his nape and flexed my fingers around his strong neck muscles.

He shivered under my touch and I smiled, hope flaring in my heart. *Fated mate...* "You mean, like soul mates or something?"

He nodded, his hands moving up to stroke my back before he held my waist with his palms. Warm tingles spread through my body wherever his skin touched mine, my muscles relaxing and turning to mush.

"Yep. We're everything you need, and you're perfect for us. I have no doubt."

I giggled, not quite sure how to respond to such an extraordinarily bold statement. Dare I listen to his silver tongue? If what he was saying was actually true, then my life had just changed forever. I wouldn't simply be a hopeless workaholic and divorcee.

I would finally have what I'd always secretly craved: a home, a husband who adored me. Maybe even children.

But could I truly trust him? What would be the cost, if he wasn't telling the truth?

My thoughts were put on hold as Jack captured my mouth with his. His lips were hot, strong, and persistent. I let my eyes slide closed and willingly gave myself up to the storm. His hand cupped my cheek and I opened my lips for his questing tongue.

Pleasure spread through my body as he took over the kiss, his lips creating magic as I pressed closer. My knees sagged and he grabbed my ass tighter, pulling me against him as our mouths stayed locked together.

I needed to feel him. *Really* feel him. He wasn't close enough.

I slid my hands down his chest and lifted the front of his shirt, breaking our kiss once I felt the heat of his skin beneath my palms. I looked down and sighed at the sight of rippled muscles.

He pulled back, lifting his arms and grabbing his shirt, and then pulled it over his head in that distinctly masculine way. Then he let it drop to the carpeted floor.

"Oh, God, you're magnificent." I breathed the words quietly, unable to stop staring. He was huge. Massive shoulders, large flat pecs, and biceps so thick I'd struggle to encircle them with both hands.

He grinned and reached for me. "As long as you like what you see."

I swallowed and nodded, overwhelmed all of a sudden.

He may be picture perfect, but I certainly wasn't.

No way was I getting undressed in front of this man. The room was far too bright, being the middle of the day plus having the lights on. The blinds were down, but I would get a reprieve from full exposure if the room was a bit darker.

"Can we turn out the lights?" I turned toward the switch, but Jack reached out to stop me.

He made *tsking* noises and shook his head as he stepped up closer. "No way. I'm not missing out on seeing you properly, this first time."

He leaned down and his hands dropped to the hem of my shirt.

I grabbed his hands, holding my top down. My heart thumped louder in my ears as the fear rose. "No, Jack. I'm not beautiful like you seem to think. Please, don't."

Litanies of my ex-husband's words came back at me in a flood.

Your ass is too big.

Your cellulite is disgusting.

You haven't even had a baby and you have stretch marks.

Tears burned the back of my eyes and throat, and I swallowed hard.

Jack straightened his spine, his height even more imposing in the small room, and a muscle jumped in his jaw as he clenched his teeth. He was upset with me now.

Damn it. Why do I always ruin everything?

"Fine, then," he said. "Have it your way, but only this time. Scott and I will want to see you. *All* of you. And you *are* beautiful. With or without clothes, I'll still think you're gorgeous."

My heart stopped for a full second as my whole body registered the shock of those words. Was he seriously upset because he *wanted* to see me naked?

He stepped away with a muttered curse and flicked the light switch and relative darkness fell.

Relief swelled as I blinked, allowing my eyes to adjust to the muted light filtering through the curtains.

"Clothes off. Now." Jack kicked off his shoes and unzipped his jeans, the scratching sound loud in the quiet room.

He pushed his pants to the floor.

I ate up the view and cursed myself for needing to hide in the shadows. I would be able to see him so much better with the lights on. His long cock was already hard, pointing toward me from between his two massive thighs.

"Ash, you need to get out of your clothes, or I'll rip them in half to get to you."

Liquid heat slid through my core and spread out between my thighs.

I want that.

Something about his desperation to get me naked was so hot. I'd never been desired like this before. Especially by a man like Jack. Beautiful, successful, sporty. He could have anyone... and he wanted *me*!

My fingers moved of their own accord, lifting up my shirt and sliding the cool cotton over my head. I let it drop to the floor and reached around my back for the bra clasp.

I had huge boobs and my ex had always said they were crude and vulgar. As I let the lacy confection drop to the floor, my breath hitched in my throat. What would Jack think of them?

His groan was carnal and almost desperate. "Fuck, you're stunning. Come here, sweetheart."

Relief was gobbled up by lust as I stepped forward. He picked me up with seeming ease and I squealed as he placed me into the center of the bed. The soft mattress at my back cushioned my body, and I stretched out my arms, eager for the man above me.

He made a growling sound as he prowled over me, his huge shoulders blocking out any remaining light as he lay on top of me.

Oh, yes.

I spread my thighs and lifted my legs to wrap around his waist, his hot belly pressing against me.

His lips found mine and he moaned, the sound shooting right through my belly. Prickles of bliss crossed my skin.

I wrapped my hands around his huge arms and held on tight as he ravaged my mouth, leaving me panting and gyrating beneath him.

He broke our kiss and I lifted my hips, waiting for the penetration that was sure to assuage this fire burning inside me. I'd never wanted a man so much.

"Fuck, you're sexy," he said, as he looked directly into my eyes before heading down my body. He kissed a line from my collarbone to my nipple, and then sucked the aching tip into his mouth with a strong pull.

"Jack!" I cried out, unable to keep the word inside.

I slid my hands into his short hair, holding him to my flesh so that he wouldn't stop. It felt so good.

He settled his full weight onto me and supported himself on his elbows as he plumped up my breast with both hands, blowing over the wet tip and making the flesh tingle before suckling the nipple deeply once again.

With a soft moan, I arched my back and let my eyes shut, half expecting him to stop and move onto something that focused on *his* pleasure. But he didn't; he simply moaned and moved over to the other side, giving my opposite breast similar attention.

A strange lethargy crept into my arms and legs. I could barely keep my legs around him. I'd never been so relaxed during sex. With my ex, he generally expected me to do most of the work, while criticizing along the way.

But with Jack I didn't need to worry if my bits were jiggling or if I was doing something wrong. He was taking control and in the best way possible. He was making my pleasure a priority. Would wonders never cease?

He pressed hot, wet kisses to my belly, seemingly unaffected by the way my tummy wobbled beneath his touch.

Then he looked up. "I can smell how aroused you are." His voice was gruff. "I can't wait to taste you."

Oh, no.... he isn't going to...

I stared down at his too-handsome face and said, "You don't have to do that. It's fine."

Jack chuckled. "Try and stop me."

Oh, my God.

I pressed both hands over my eyes. I couldn't watch.

Wet sensation flicked across my clit and I cried out, involuntarily arching up to meet the foreign feeling. More pressure followed as he ran his tongue between my folds and around my clit. Up and down and around, creating flickers of fire that spread through my body, centering low in my belly.

He pressed his face in and inhaled deeply, his groan vibrating against my skin. "Fuck, you smell divine."

I frowned, disappointment cutting through me. I'd hoped Jack wouldn't lie to me.

I opened my mouth to argue, but he thrust his tongue deep inside my pussy. I cried out, my back arching high as a wave of pleasure crashed over me.

I thrust my breasts higher, running my hands over them and tweaking my nipples to increase the pleasure as he pressed my thighs open farther with his large palms.

He moved his tongue back up to my clit, the swollen bud shooting tingles of ecstasy through me as he began to suckle on it.

Well, he'd proved one major thing to me. Some men really did like eating pussy. But I needed so much more, and the need was clawing at my core.

"Oh, for the love of...Jack!" I sat up, grabbed at his head, and pulled on his hair. "Come up here. Make love to me."

I was more than ready. My legs were restless and tight, my pussy was empty and aching for him.

He looked up from between my legs, his blue eyes turning almost black in passion. "No. I want you to come on my tongue before I take you."

"But I..." *I can't do that.*

I collapsed back on the bed as he latched onto my clit and began to suckle it, hard.

I arched and shifted my legs, panting and tossing my head to get some hold on reality. My mind was splintering apart. No man had ever made me come in this way, and I'd never come this quickly at all. Period. I wasn't sure I could.

But Jack didn't stop. He slid his tongue down my seam and began fucking me with his tongue. I screamed and grabbed for his head again, gripping his hair and holding him to me as the wave began to gather speed.

My belly tightened and pleasure curled inside me until I panted. His fingers teased my opening, and then slid into my tightness, and the ecstatic feelings inside me doubled in intensity.

He flicked my clit with an action like butterfly wings—fast and intense. I cried out. This was too much.

But he didn't stop. He just continued to flick his tongue over and over the swollen flesh until I couldn't hold back anymore and began to come.

"Jack...oh, fuck!" I gasped as my orgasm crested, all the air going out of my lungs as time ceased to exist for one perfect moment, and then my belly seized and began to spasm. Jack's hands held my thighs apart as waves of pleasure pummelled into me.

I screamed, feeling my inner passages convulse around his

fingers as sensation exploded from my clit, moving through my body in wave upon wave of sensation.

When the tremors finally stopped, I lay flat, my eyes closed and feeling so heavy I had no hope of opening them at all. Heat tingled behind my eyelids as two tears slipped free and slid down my face.

I lifted my hands and wiped them away discreetly, amazed at the sheer joy within. I'd never known my body could feel like that.

Jack was humming and still lapping at my skin, his fingers moving in and out of me. "You taste even better than I imagined."

I needed him closer. Deeper. Inside me.

I forced my eyes open, sat up, and reached down to run my hands over the beautiful hot skin of his back. "Come here, honey."

He looked up and his eyes were gold in the dim light. I blinked a few times and shook my head. I was probably seeing things.

"You want me to come up to you?" he asked.

I laughed and nodded, tugging on his shoulders. "Please."

He crawled up and lay on his side, staring at me with a bewildered look. His eyes were a dark blue again.

It must have been my imagination.

He rested his hand on my tummy and I shuffled closer. He was being so stiff, and I wasn't sure why he didn't want to be closer.

Maybe he wasn't a cuddler?

I turned my head and smelled his skin, the faint sweet scent making me extend my tongue and lick his strong shoulder.

Hmm....

"Don't you want to sleep?" he asked, and I shook my head, rolling over so that he could spoon me if he wanted to. I loved the feel of his strength engulfing me.

I didn't want to sleep, but if he wanted to rest before I touched him too, I could handle that. "Cuddle, please."

He settled in behind me and pressed his lips to my ear. "I can't believe you still want to touch me when you've already come."

What?

I jerked, and then twisted around so I could look at him.

He did not just say that. Who the hell has this man been sleeping with?

I stared at him and let the surprise settle within me. I needed to remember that this handsome man had some scars of his own.

Jack

I LOOKED DOWN at the most beautiful woman I'd ever seen and couldn't understand why she was staring at me in what appeared to be shock or maybe outrage.

"Of course, I want to touch you," she said. "You just gave me the most beautiful experience of my life."

Pride flooded through me. I grinned and kissed the tip of Ash's nose.

I appreciated the compliment, but that hadn't stopped the women I'd been with in the past from turning over and falling asleep without a backward glance.

I kissed her lips, closing my eyes, and a strange noise escaped my throat. Was that really me making all those moaning noises? I'd thought it was her originally, but I could hear it clearly now.

And it wasn't Ash.

She slipped her tongue into my mouth, and her sweetness sent a jolt of pleasure through my body. Every muscle shivered in anticipation of our mating.

She pushed me back a little so I broke the kiss, a frown marring her exquisite face. "Seriously, what did you mean by that?"

I smiled down at my lover, an amazing feeling of relaxation passing over me. My eyes were heavy, and my shoulders were releasing their stress.

God, I feel good.

"I mean...most women just use me to gain a release," I said. "But you're not, are you? You honestly want *me*."

She nodded, redness coloring her face. "Of course, I want you!

You're amazing! Generous, selfless, confident, funny! I've only known you for one day and I already feel closer to you than I do some of the people I've known all my life."

She picked up one of my hands and pressed a kiss to my rough palm, the touch of her soft lips erasing the pain of those past moments of so-called intimacy I'd had with others.

"Thank you, sweetheart." My voice was rough. I cleared my throat with an embarrassed cough. I captured her chin in my hand and held her face while I rained kisses down on her soft skin—her cheek, her nose, her forehead, and those lips that were sweeter than the purest honey. "I'm going to love you so well, you'll never leave me, Ash."

She gasped against my lips and I pulled back, my brain stuttering over the words I'd said.

Before today, I'd only told one woman in my life that I loved her —my ex-wife.

And look how that turned out.

But this was the first time it felt right. It hadn't been true, pure love before.

Ash's face began to transform. The cloud that had been hovering over her eyes disappeared, leaving behind a clear beauty. Her blue eyes lit up and a smile like the summer sunshine broke across her face.

She began to laugh, and I lay there and watched. Tears leaked down her face as she let go of whatever terrible thing she'd been holding on to.

When she finally stopped chortling, she wiped the tears away and looked at me with a warm expression bordering on wonder. "Why do I actually believe you?"

I growled and rolled on top of her, pinning her gorgeous body and settling between her thighs. "Because I never lie."

And I was going to prove it, every day. For the rest of my life.

If only I could work out a way to get Scott to fall into line...

SIX

JACK

I bent my head to suck on Ash's neck, loving the feel of her heartbeat fluttering beneath my lips.

I couldn't claim her today, I knew I couldn't without Scott here too... but the need rode me hard. My shifter was practically doing laps of anxiety inside my head.

Despite Scott's reservations about the whole perfect pair mating thing, the legends were true. I could feel it with every fiber of my being.

We needed Ash and would never be happy without her.

How she would take that was a whole other issue.

"How are you feeling about the idea of being both my and Scott's mate?" I asked.

She frowned and lifted her hand, using her fingertips to make circles on my shoulder. "I don't really know, to be honest. If you'd asked me last week how I felt about threesomes, I would have been horrified at the very idea of it. But having seen my cousin with her two husbands, and knowing a bit better how the dynamics of it all works, thanks to you... I..."

Color bloomed in her cheeks. Ah, so she was struggling with the fact that she didn't mind the idea now.

Women were so bloody contradictory.

"All I'm asking, Ash, is for you to keep an open mind about it," I said, lifting her hand and kissing her knuckles. "I know in theory it seems strange, but I have faith in the legends of my people."

She cocked her head. "Your people?"

"Mmhmm." I hummed and began kissing her again, not wanting to reveal all our secrets yet. It would be hard enough to convince her to accept both of us at once, let alone understand the fact that we both turned into mountain lions whenever we felt like it.

"My turn," Ash said as she wiggled out from beneath me and pushed on my chest as though she wanted me to roll off her.

"Huh?" I followed her lead and lay on my back beside her.

She kissed down my chest, her soft, wet lips giving me gentle shocks against my skin. Her tongue flicked out and licked one of my nipples, and lightning zinged through my chest.

"Hey, come up here, beautiful girl," I said, reaching down to pull her up to me. I was uncomfortable but not quite sure why. I just needed her to stop giving me so much attention. She glared at me. "No, I want to touch you too, Jack."

I chuckled and lay my hand over hers where it gripped my bicep. "You are."

She shook her head. "No, I mean I want to be able to enjoy your incredible body without you distracting me or stopping me."

My face heated and for the first time I was glad for the dimly lit room. "You don't have to pay me back, Ash. I'd prefer just to pleasure you."

And I honestly did. Why was she acting so strangely about that?

She giggled and moved to my other nipple, this time sucking it into her mouth. I gasped as my cock twitched against my thigh.

It didn't make sense that such a simple thing could feel so good.

She continued to move down my body, kissing my torso, and I instinctively sucked in my gut. I was getting a bit thick in the waist; perhaps I'd start running again since I now had her to impress.

As if she could sense my sudden lack of confidence, she gently smacked my belly. "You have the most magnificent body I have ever seen in real life." She punctuated her words with slow kisses over my abs.

I laughed, shaking my head a little. "As long as you want what you see, sweetheart, I'm happy."

She looked up and gave me a big smile, the sort that made me clench my teeth against the urgent desire that had my cock surging upward. She was too beautiful—inside and out.

Where have you been all my life?

She moved down and before I realized what she had planned, she took my already-excited cock into her mouth.

I hissed through my teeth as she wrapped her hot fist around the base and sucked the sensitive head into her mouth, sending hot streams of sensation through my cock and into my body.

"Oh, wow, that feels wonderful." I forced my eyes open as I watched her work. Feeling the wet heat and suction was hot enough, but looking down at her was the most erotic thing I'd ever seen.

Ash, my mate, and the most beautiful, intelligent woman I'd ever met, had chosen to take my cock in her mouth. She *actually* wanted to give me attention.

She flicked her tongue out and licked the slit, pulling a groan from my throat and clenching my hands into fists. My orgasm teased at me, my balls tightening and drawing up against my body.

I held on to my control by my fingernails, enjoying the fight inside my body as her beautiful mouth licked and teased me.

She began moving her hand as well, squeezing the shaft and stroking my cock as she sucked.

The heat began to move over me like a wave and I grabbed at her hands. "Stop, stop."

I tried to pull away, but she gripped the shaft harder, pulled her mouth off with a wet *pop,* and pinned me with a glare. "Why?"

Tendrils of pleasure licked at me, threatening to overwhelm me. "I don't want to come like this. I'll wait until tonight...or until I can be inside you. It's better if we wait a bit longer to make love, I think."

I practiced the principles of Tantric, usually, and didn't mind pulling myself back from an orgasm. But it was more than that. I wanted to come with her pussy wrapped around my cock, and the wait would be worth it.

She continued to stroke me with her hand. "Why should we wait? Don't you want me?"

"Ah…" *Trees, water, ice.* I pulled up as many images of non-arousing things as I could think of, rather than the picture she made with her hand around my cock and her tempting mouth oh-so-close.

"Of course, I want you," I said. "You're fucking gorgeous. But if you really want to be a family with my twin and I, the legends encourage the first mating to be with all three of us together."

Oh, fuck. You idiot! Stop talking her out of it. She wants you.

I panted and gasped as she kept her perfect stroking pace going.

"I suppose that makes sense," she said, "as much as any of this does."

She kissed the crown of my cock in goodbye. The traitor wept a pearl of white precum out the tip as another wave of arousal crashed into me again.

Then she smiled with a slightly wicked cast. "No, I don't think so. If we can't have sex, then I want you to come now. Like this."

She engulfed my cock in one movement and the pleasure picked me up and threw me against the shore.

"Oh, fuck!" I cried out and made one last attempt to pull away, but she held on tight as I began to orgasm. White lights flashed in front of my eyes and sweat broke out across my forehead as hot cum spilled out of me. My entire body shuddered with pleasure.

Amazingly, she swallowed me down, continuing to lick and hum happily, her throat rippling around me.

My orgasmic shivers continued, vibrating along my arms and legs. "Oh, wow. Oh, wow."

My brain was stuck on a loop.

She let my softening flesh slip from her mouth and began kissing a pattern back up to my face. My arms were heavy, but I forced them to rise and wrap around her warm body as she settled against me and kissed my chest.

Bliss descended, making me black out several times before my body finally relaxed. I chuckled, unable to keep my happiness inside. "Thank you, sweetheart."

I'd given her every opportunity to be selfish and only take from me. And instead, she'd given as good as she'd gotten.

More so. And that was a first for me.

I kissed the top of her head, smiling against her strawberry-scented hair. "Do you want to hang out tonight? We could get some dinner later, maybe try to pin Scott down?"

She nodded and hummed, nestling into my side and relaxing against me.

I glanced over to the clock across the room. It was only three thirty. "Maybe a nap first?" I rolled to the side and drew her body flush against me.

Her breath fluttered against my chest as she nuzzled into my shoulder. "Yes, please."

I let my body relax and sink down into the darkness. For the first time in my life, a soul-deep happiness fell over me, wrapping me in its warmth.

Scott

I blinked my eyes open, groaning as the late-morning sun hit my overtired body. My shoulders hurt, my quads were tight, and my head was so foggy I could barely manage one clunky thought at a time.

I'd barely slept a wink last night, which was bad even for me. I usually managed at least a couple of hours of solid sleep, but last night I'd tossed and turned, even reaching down to stroke myself to orgasm around five in the morning, hoping the lethargy would knock me out. *No such luck.* I'd seen every minute of the clock tick over until seven and must have fallen asleep after that.

I ached everywhere and if I hadn't been in perfect health last night, I'd think I was coming down with a virus of some sort.

"Oh, for fuck's sake," I muttered.

I couldn't ignore the pain in my lower abdomen a moment longer. I rolled out of bed and staggered to the toilet, my head pounding with a persistent headache and my knees shaking as they struggled to carry my weight after no rest overnight.

I growled and stretched in front of the mirror, noticing the black circles beneath my eyes. "Bloody Jack."

Something was up with my twin. I'd only felt this terrible a few times in my life, and it was always linked to something massive happening to Jack.

Stupid damn mystical twin connection.

Was something threatening him?

I showered and dried myself, my lion pushing up at me for a run. It'd been so long since I'd let my animal shifter loose. Probably too long to be healthy.

I glanced at my wardrobe and decided against getting dressed. Instead, I focused on my tingling body and opened the back door. It was time to embrace my lion.

I let go of my humanity and allowed my shifter to take over.

Cinnamon fur sprouted over my skin and I dropped to all fours as my body and face transformed into my mountain lion.

The wild animal itself was quite a loner, but my shifter family was closely knitted together, liking the comfort of others above the solitary existence of a real cougar.

The wind rustled my fur as I took a deep breath through my nose, smelling the fresh scent of spring: the rich dirt and the crisp leaves, together with the promise of a light rain.

I let a loud growl rumble through my body as I bounded down

the back steps and raced into the fragrant woods. It had been so long since I'd run like this, experiencing the world through these eyes. I'd forgotten how beautiful it was. My heart was lighter and happier from being in animal form. I was free and healthy. There was a lot to be thankful for.

For safety and space, all my family lived near the base of the mountains. My brother and I were no exception. Another strange twinge moved through my heart. Something wasn't right with my brother. I had to get to him.

I turned and ran toward Jack's home, not quite a mile from my own house. I couldn't shake the feeling that something was very wrong.

I reached the property in minutes. I rounded the small weatherboard home and stopped short, my paws sliding in the dirt. My heart pounded in my chest.

Jack wasn't home.

His truck wasn't parked in the driveway where it was every morning. He could be at the gym, but it was Saturday—the one day Jack would normally sleep in.

I supposed Jack could have slept over with one of his lovers, but that was highly unlikely, especially since he'd laid eyes on Ash and decided she was our mate. Even without Ash in the mix, he didn't do sleepovers. He preferred his own bed.

I turned and headed home, my brain churning over the possibilities.

Could he be hurt? No. It'd be something simple. Maybe he'd gone somewhere with the kids?

I jumped up onto my back patio and shook my fur to rid myself of the excess dirt. My belly was jumpy and churning, the unease I'd been feeling all morning settling in like a permanent scar.

I purred as my mind focused, my humanity returning to help my brain realize the obvious as I returned to human form.

Jack's with her. Ash.

I knew it in my bones.

My stomach clenched and I ran inside. I panted and paced my sleek kitchen. I couldn't do anything about the situation now. Jack had wanted her, despite my feelings about it all. And that was his choice.

Instead of giving my anger anymore thought, I threw myself into my work, doing some online research and reading the latest journals. That was, until the need to get up and move became impossible to ignore. I ate lunch and paced once again, grinding my teeth.

Jack, Jack. Fucking Jack!

I snatched up my cell phone and scowled at the screen. He could not be with Ash, he couldn't. Not when he knew what finding our mate would mean for me.

"Of course, he bloody can," I said to myself. "Bloody man whore..."

We'd decided not to go after her... hadn't we? Or was that just me?

My heart kicked out with such a sickening thud that my knees weakened.

I staggered to my couch and fell onto the soft leather with a groan.

This was so... unfair. All of it.

Ash was *our mate.* And yet, Jack was the one who had the balls to go after her.

No!

"*Fuck!*" I stretched out the word with a growl. Then, I looked up and yelled wordlessly at the ceiling before punching in his number on my phone. The anger inside me grew.

I'd gone through twenty years of hell with a woman. I wasn't stupid enough to trust another one, and my brother was an idiot for thinking it would be better this time.

I blew air out my nose as the call connected, not caring that in the mood I was in, I was going to rip Jack's head off, no matter where he was.

"Scott?" Jack sounded groggy, his tone filled with confusion.

"Where are you?" I snapped.

"I can hear you just fine at a lower decibel," he said. "I'm with Ash. Where else would I be?"

Hot, angry waves poured over me like a never-ending ocean of feeling. It was too much, pulling me under and drowning me in pain. I took a quick, sharp breath and clenched my jaw. "You fucked her already? God, Jack, you don't waste any time, do you?"

Silence descended after a distinctively feminine gasp sounded over the line.

"I'll call you later," was all Jack said, before he promptly hung up on me.

The background noise whirling inside my angry mind stopped.

And I began to shake.

I pushed myself to my feet and rushed toward the kitchen, making it just in time to feel the burn of stomach acid clearing my throat and spilling into the sink.

I retched several times, salty hot tears stinging my eyes while I took deep breaths through my nose in an attempt to calm down.

Sweat broke out over my body as alternating waves of hot and cold flowed through me.

When my stomach had stopped clenching with painful contractions, I splashed some water onto my face and swirled it around my mouth before spitting it out. Then I sank to the floor, the cold tiles jolting me when my palms came into contact.

I coughed, my lungs seizing for a moment before resuming their wheezing.

My head slumped forward and I concentrated solely on breathing.

So, my twin was with our mate, a woman we both had decided didn't exist.

I wanted to believe the attraction I was feeling... the rightness of the situation, that it was true this time. And a small part of me did. The other, larger part was terrified. The scientist in me was baffled and critical of the alleged bond, despite feeling the connection between us as though it were a physical thing.

I had to get up.

I forced myself to my feet, my legs like lead beneath me. I dragged my feet along the corridor and threw myself into the shower, blasting my sluggish body with cold water.

"Fuck! Shit!" I yelled as I jumped from foot to foot, the freezing water like needles against my skin, knocking any lingering lethargy from my body.

After I washed, I stepped out of the cubicle and began toweling myself dry.

Ash and Jack had fucked. Mated. Whatever the hell our kind did with the woman meant for them. I had to get used to that fact.

Jack had taken the opportunity to pursue her, to bond with her, and if she was as smart as she seemed, she'd jump at the chance to be with my fun, good-looking, kind-hearted brother. But where did that leave me?

"Between a rock and a hard place in the middle of fucking nowhere, that's where," I said to my reflection in the bathroom mirror.

I dressed, my head swimming from a lack of food and too much stress. Sadly, that state of affairs wasn't unusual with the way my life had gone.

I had to make a choice.

Either watch Jack be with Ash and be happy for them, or get over my fear and join them. And of course, that was contingent on the fact that she'd forgive me for what I'd said to Jack on the phone.

I was certain of one thing, though: I couldn't lose my brother's love due to envy. The three of us being together was how it was supposed to be.

I'd studied Brandon and Tyler during their bonding ceremony and knew it to be true.

But I was too broken to be part of a relationship, especially one as perfect as a truly mated perfect pair with their soul mate should be.

Wasn't I?

I called myself three types of a fool as anger toward my brother rolled in my gut. I should never have picked up the phone. What on earth had possessed me?

I rolled onto my side and smiled at Ash as well as I could with the weight of dread on my chest. "I'm sorry about that."

Her blue eyes glowed with hurt as she turned away, her breathing rate increasing.

I stifled a groan of frustration and snuggled up behind her, the heat of her back radiating against my chest, and hissed in pleasure as she huffed out a sigh and wiggled closer.

Thank God for that.

"He sounded angry." Her voice was small in the room as she ran her fingernails up and down the arm I'd slung over her belly.

I shivered as the hairs on my arm stuck up and a wave of pleasure pulsed through me. "God, I love your touch."

She didn't say anything, but she seemed to relax more against me. I kissed the whorl of her ear, my cock throbbing against her soft bottom.

"I told you he wouldn't react well," I said in a low voice. "His heart's taken a real beating in the past."

She made a *hmmph* noise and rolled onto her back, staring up at me with wide, clear eyes. "Is that really all I am to you, Jack? A fuck?"

I groaned and tried not to roll my eyes. "You know that's not what you are to me. Even Scott knows it. If it was just that, he wouldn't be so upset. The fact that it's so much more than that is why he was such a prick."

She flicked my chest with her thumb and middle finger. "I'm not stupid, you know. Did you make up all that crap about the three of us being together? Spin me a pretty tale to beat your brother to the punch?"

Her mouth turned down and her eyes glistened with tears.

Whoa, she was hurt, or angry, or both.

My gut churned at the idea that I'd upset her in any way. I'd always been a bit clueless with women, but I'd worked out a long time ago that honesty was always the best policy.

"Sweetheart, stop jumping to the wrong conclusions," I said. "I promise you I won't lie to you. Everything I've said is true, and my idiot brother is so jealous at the moment he can't see straight."

Ash stared off into the distance and dug her nails rhythmically into my forearm. "Then why would he say such a thing?"

I gently grabbed her chin and tilted her face back to me. "Because he's damaged, beautiful. He wants your love so much he can taste it, but he's terrified. He lashed out because he's being ridden by the green-eyed monster, and that's not pretty."

She stopped her agitated movements and began to stroke my arms again.

I held my breath as emotions I couldn't identify flickered across her face.

Finally, she heaved a sigh and stared up at me. "So, what are we going to do about it then?"

Relief flooded my soul. Her can-do attitude proved to me once again why she was my fated mate.

I laughed and kissed her cute, button nose. She was all heart, but with a fire that Scott and I both needed. "So, you want to try to get him to join us, too, huh?"

She looked down, her expression shuttered as her eyebrows lowered. I watched her and waited, counting my heartbeats. She bit her lower lip, worrying the flesh with her teeth.

Please, don't say no, beautiful.

When she finally glanced up, her eyes had darkened and a smile flirted at the edge of her full lips. "I think I do. If you guys come as a set, it would be silly to only collect one."

I burst out laughing and drew her against me for a kiss, tasting the sweetness of her mouth with my tongue.

When the mood shifted into something hotter, I reluctantly pulled away and extricated myself from her clinging arms. "Well, sweetheart, if that's what you truly want, then I better go home and get dressed for our dinner date. Shall I invite my brother to join us?"

Her gaze darted around and she bit her lip as she held on tight to the blanket that covered her naked body. Eventually she nodded. "Yes."

Relief coursed through me like a cold rain. I rolled off the mattress and stood next to the bed, my shoulders relaxed. "I'll call that idiot brother of mine and set up our date."

Ash giggled and nodded again, pleasure written all over her face.

A soft growl surfaced as I surveyed the picture in front of me. She was like the goddess Aphrodite—all luscious curves and womanly beauty hidden only by a thin sheet.

"You are so tempting," I said. "I want to climb back into that bed and have my way with you."

She pushed the blanket down to her waist and came up on her elbows, her bountiful and soft breasts now fully on display.

I grinned. "Oh, you vixen."

I wasn't ignoring that open invitation.

I fell back onto the bed and grabbed both breasts with my hands, suckling on one delicious nipple and then the other, my body already hard in response to the mewling sounds she made.

Fuck! I won't be able to stop this time.

Breathing hard, my balls aching and my cock hard, I slowly crawled off the bed and with jerky movements grabbed for my clothes.

"I already want you so bad, Ash, but if we're gonna do this right, then we better wait a bit longer. Yeah?"

She nodded, her face flushed with passion.

Waiting was the right thing to do, but if Scott didn't get his act together super-fast, I'd take her for myself without hesitation.

I pulled on my jeans, being careful not to catch my still-hard cock in the zipper before I moved on to button my shirt. "I'll pick you up about six, okay?"

"Yeah, that'd be great. But how are you and I going to act in front of Scott?" she asked.

I sat in the single chair against the wall and tugged on my boots. I hadn't really thought about that. "Natural, I guess. You're mine no matter what my twin decides, so whatever you're comfortable with is fine by me."

She gave me a huge smile, and hot honey swept through my belly.

God, I already love her.

I crossed the room and knelt by the bed for another quick kiss, her taste bursting through me and making me purr. "I'll see you soon."

When I pulled back, Ash was giggling. "Why do you make those weird noises sometimes?"

I fought the blush down as my cheeks heated. *Because my mountain lion is happy in your presence.* "I'll tell you some other time. Let's get Scott in line first, if that's okay?"

I'd told her the truth; a lie by omission wasn't really a lie, was it?

Ash shrugged and settled back into the pillows. "Okay, Jack."

I winked and tore myself away before I could forget the objective of waiting for Scott to join us. After blowing her a kiss, I exited the room and then bounced out to my car. I jumped into the cabin, feeling happier than I had in decades. I had a future and I was going to be happy.

Now, if I could just convince my twin to get with the program.

I dialed his number.

On the second ring, he picked up. "Hello?"

His tone was sheepish, and although part of me wanted to reprimand him for the conversation this morning, I had a bigger goal in mind.

"Hey, Scott," I said, as if nothing had happened. "You free for dinner?"

"Yeah. Why?"

"The two of us need to spend some time with Ash."

"I don't want to, and I certainly don't *need* to."

I rolled my eyes and pressed the phone closer to my ear. It was time to push my brother outside his comfort zone. We didn't have unlimited time with Ash, and I wanted it sorted out before she had to go home.

"Well, I'm already in love with the woman and if you were any sort of brother, you'd at least want to meet her for more than a few minutes and get to know her," I said.

A soft growl came through the phone, and I grinned.

Pushing his jealousy button may not be the best way to go, but calling on Scott's family integrity would definitely get his attention.

I continued. "I know you're not interested in being a three-part family, but Ash is awesome and I want her in my life. Forever."

Another strangled noise and a huff. "Still don't see why I have to see her."

Strange butterflies whipped around my belly at the strain in my brother's voice. Scott was confused, and that meant he was thinking things over.

Thank God for that.

We were destined to love Ash together. I knew it all the way to my bones. We'd been wrong, so wrong, about everything. Scott and I had gone against our fate, believing we knew better, and we'd paid dearly.

I clenched my teeth and let out a soft whine.

Yes, we'd fucked up, but we'd found our mate now and she needed more than just me. Scott and I were a perfect pair, designed to love one woman and give her everything she needed.

If Scott wasn't with us, Ash would never truly be fully satisfied.

I took a breath and exhaled. "Because you're my brother. If I convince her that I need her, she'll be moving here. I want you to be a part of our lives, and besides...aren't you at least a tad curious?"

He huffed and puffed, and then went quiet. Finally, he said, "Okay, I'll join you guys for dinner. But don't expect anything more than that, Jack. I'm happy as I am."

Bullshit.

I grinned so wide my cheeks ached. "I know, bro. See you at O'Meara's at six thirty."

Scott

I stood on the nature strip outside the restaurant and sucked in a deep breath through my mouth. I let it out slowly, my shoulders sagging from their position up near my ears.

My heart beat a sickening rhythm, and a strange swirl was making my belly sick. I didn't want to do this.

I glanced in through the glass door of the only nice restaurant in Trenthy and something akin to a two-by-four smacked me squarely in the gut.

There she is.

Everything inside me relaxed and purred, my lion happy with Fate's choice.

My gaze practically devoured her healthy, glowing skin and the smile she gave my brother who sat across the table from her.

Could I really do this? Meet Ash as my brother's girlfriend...and then walk away.

Get some balls, would you! Or did Kerry remove them completely?

I stiffened my resolve, shook my head, and reached for the door handle. Deep down, I knew I wouldn't be able to walk away once I got to know her, and that was my biggest fear.

My hand shook as I pulled open the door and stepped over the threshold, the brightly lit room making me blink as I took another deep breath to calm the racing of my heart.

After my horrendous marriage finally ended, I'd been certain I'd spend the rest of my life alone. Jack and I had already agreed that our fated mate didn't exist. I probably still would be alone, of course, but I'd been wrong about one thing.

Our fated mate was most definitely real.

There was no doubt in my mind now.

With each step I took through the restaurant, my thigh muscles flexed and shook a little more.

As I walked closer to Ash, the inevitability of my future came barrelling at me, like a river breaking its banks and flowing over new land.

Was this really going to be my life now?

This wasn't how I'd planned it. Part of me wanted to hold on to my pain forever. That might have sounded stupid if I said it aloud, but pain was all I knew these days. It kept me safe; it was the space where I was most comfortable.

I stepped up to the table, my skin slick with a sheen of sweat as Ash turned toward me. Her quick intake of breath and the lust swirling in her eyes made me want to sink to my knees and thank whatever supreme being had sent her my way.

Oh, God. This is worse than I thought it would be.

"Hi, Scott." Her voice was husky and soothing, yet warm and welcoming.

I swallowed past the lump in my throat and rubbed at the aching spot on my chest where my heart was kicking out. I'd never believed in love at first sight, but God, if there was such a thing, this was it.

"Sit down." Jack pulled out a chair next to him, and I fell into it, absurdly having to blink away hot tears as Ash continued to smile at me like I'd just come home from a long stint away.

I coughed and cleared my throat, picking up the menu lying on the table in front of me.

Cool, stay cool. You have no idea if she even wants you as her second mate.

"You guys ordered yet?" I asked without looking up.

Jack swivelled around from the chair next to me and slid onto the booth next to Ash, his arm moving around her with familiarity as he pulled her close.

I held my breath and almost groaned as she settled against him, her gaze flicking up to his face with a smile before turning back to me.

Oh, that's right. They're dating, and I'm just the third wheel. Fuck!

"No, we were waiting for you. I've never been here before. Can you recommend anything, Scott?" I heard the smile in her voice as I stared back down at the printed words on the white paper.

My eyes kept crossing, which made it impossible to read. I breathed deep through my nose as I fought with the molten jealousy that had begun to flow through me.

"Ah…" I made humming noises as I struggled with my breathing, my throat closing up on me.

Jack spoke in my stead. "The steak's good, but I haven't tried much else."

I looked up then, and he grinned. The bloody caveman wouldn't eat much else.

"The white wine risotto is nice and so is the salmon. Or the duck." I glanced at Ash and forced the red haze from my brain. I could be happy for my brother. I could…

Yeah, with the one woman designed for me, too!

I frowned and called a waiter over. I couldn't even control my own thoughts at the moment. "Can we get some drinks?"

The waiter nodded and pulled out his pad and pen.

"I'll have a glass of Cab Sauv. Ash?" I clenched my teeth so tightly together pain splintered along my jaw.

Jack had his lips pressed against hers, his hand cupping her face with a reverence that was almost beautiful to watch.

Almost...

I glared back at the waiter, who looked down to avoid my gaze.

"I'll have the chicken risotto. No mushrooms, extra Parmesan."

"Ash, honey," Jack said, parting from her at last. "What would you like?"

I forced my gaze back to them.

"I'll have a glass of chardonnay and the duck, please," she said, with a smile at the waiter.

She took my recommendation. Good choice.

Jack tapped the menu. "Steak, medium rare and a beer, thanks."

Typical.

The waiter left and I concentrated on my body. Breath flowed in and out. I linked my fingers in my lap and forced the tight muscles in my arms to relax.

With a deep breath, I asked, "What did you guys do today?"

I could do this. I'd made my choice. Told Jack I didn't want her... now I had to man up and live with that decision. Ash grinned and looked up at Jack, the color in her cheeks making her shine even brighter. "We just stayed in bed for the morning, mostly. Talked about life, past crap, everything and anything."

Flutters of unease rippled through my belly as I looked between my brother and Ash. They wouldn't have discussed me, would they?

"Past stories?" I forced a smile to my face and some humor into my voice. "Like the football games Jack led to victory?"

Ash smiled and leaned against Jack. She had obviously been intimate with him already.

Acid burned in my gut so badly I had to lay a hand on my belly to still the spasms.

"Yeah, but more important stuff than that. If I really am the person that Fate designed for you two..." She stopped and my heart jumped in my chest. "I'm sorry. I mean, for Jack, I suppose...anyway... then I want to know about the good *and* the bad."

My heart thumped so hard it made me sick every time it hit my ribs.

"Like what?" My voice squeaked, and I coughed.

The waiter delivered our drinks, and I lifted my glass in desperation for something liquid in my throat.

Jack leaned forward and lifted his beer. "To new beginnings and to you, Ash. You are a godsend, my beautiful girl."

Ash blushed and clinked her glass with his, and then turned to do the same with mine.

I couldn't think properly; everything was moving in slow motion. I nodded and drank half the glass in one swallow.

The peppery liquid slid down my throat and I shook my head to clear the regret floating around the cavernous space.

"What did you get up to today?" Jack asked me, his eyebrows flicking up.

I shrugged, feeling my lion rising within me, needing another run. "Nothing much. Went for a run, did some work."

Our meals were served, and my stomach rumbled as the sweet chicken scent filled my nostrils. I dug into it, reveling in each bite. It had to be one of my favorite dishes.

As my stomach filled and my body relaxed, I could breathe a little easier.

"So, tell me about your work, Scott," Ash said. "Jack was hopeless at explaining what you do."

I rolled my eyes at my brother, who shrugged and kept eating his huge lump of meat. "I do research for the government."

I picked up my glass and took the last sip of wine, savoring the taste of the red while the warmth of it swilled around my palate and down my throat.

"What sort of research?" she asked.

I froze, and then slowly placed my glass on the table. No one had ever asked me a question past the initial one. In fact, my answer usually ended the conversation. Who wanted to know about boring research, especially when my brother, the footballer and coach, was around?

"Genetic research into the origins of cellular memory and possible uses of junk DNA."

Her eyes lit up and she straightened in her seat. "Really? That is awesome! Tell me more."

I stared at her in shock for a moment, taking in her excited features. She *really* wanted to know? I couldn't tell her too much because my sector was being funded by the government, but I could tell her *some* things.

I began talking about my work, giving her more details than I'd ever given anyone, because she was the only one who'd ever pushed for a real answer.

She asked intelligent questions and knew a lot more cellular autonomy than I'd thought a pharmacist would.

The waiter came and cleared away our plates, and Jack drew Ash back into the circle of his arms. She smiled a little stiffly, flicking her eyes back and forth before settling against his side.

A heavy weight pressed against my chest as I watched Jack's fingers slide up and down her bare arm.

The waiter came back with a smile. "Would you like to order some coffees?"

I shook my head and glanced back at the beautiful woman staring at me with massive blue eyes and the fullest lips I'd ever seen.

Jack grinned. "You wanna come back to my place for another drink?"

Air whistled through my teeth as I inhaled sharply. I nodded before I could talk myself out of this stupid decision and stood up, not quite sure what I'd do when it was just the three of us in a room and nowhere to hide.

The attraction to Ash was so intense it was going to be almost impossible to stay away from her if I had the opportunity to touch her. What would she taste like?

My mountain lion purred within me and I forced my shaking legs forward to the front of the restaurant to pay.

If Ashleigh was my destiny, shouldn't I put myself to the ultimate test?

It was only fair.

And then I would make the final decision.

EIGHT

JACK

I drove Ash back to my place, my lion practically dancing inside me with excitement. As I pulled into my driveway, my skin tingled and my muscles bulged with the effort to keep my strong animal contained. I'd made the decision not to join with my mate last night, or this morning. Without the other half of my perfect pair, it hadn't felt right. Ash was made for both of us and none would feel complete unless all three of us mated together.

I inhaled sharply, my breath skimming over my teeth. I had faith that Fate would pull it all together for us when, in a few minutes, I'd have them both in my bedroom.

A grin spread across my face as happiness flooded through me, like sunshine blessing the ground with its kiss as it rose each morning.

In the passenger seat, Ash fidgeted with her fingers. "Do you really think Scott wants me? It doesn't seem like it. Not at all."

I laughed as Scott's car pulled up behind us, my belly rippling with a real humor I hadn't felt in a decade. This beautiful woman could not still be so insecure, surely? My brother's need for her was as clear as fresh spring water.

I patted her thigh. "Oh, he wants you, sweetheart, so bad he's sweating bullets."

"What do you mean?"

I laughed again. "Scott is trying to work out how to get away from us tonight before he reveals the truth and jumps on you."

She gave a high-pitched, nervous laugh. I stepped out of the car and joined her when she exited, pulling her into my arms as we headed to the front door. Scott's car door slammed as he got out, and I dropped my head and claimed Ash's mouth. Her honeyed sweetness tempted me as I licked along the seam of her lips before delving between them.

Scott cleared his throat loudly behind us, and Ash stiffened in my arms.

I tightened my hold on her to reassure her that I wasn't going anywhere, and then eased back. I dropped a kiss on her nose before finally turning away to open the door.

Like most of my family, I owned a home close to the base of the Rockies, with a substantial parcel of land around it. The location made it safer for us, not to mention convenient, when we needed to shift and run. Our animals didn't belong in a cage, no matter how comfortable.

"Come on in," I said, gesturing her to follow me.

I walked down the narrow hallway and into the small kitchen. I smiled to myself as I heard the front door close, so I pulled open the fridge.

"You wanna beer, Scott?" I called. "I've got some white wine if you'd like some, Ash?"

She said, "Yeah, thanks, Jack. That'd be great."

I turned to watch my brother and our woman eye each other from the doorway. He nodded slowly in response to my question.

The atmosphere was tense but in the best way, with sexual heat and tension.

I grinned and grabbed two beers and the wine. When was Scott going to admit that he really did want the love we'd both been denied all our lives?

When would he acknowledge that he actually *deserved* love, not pain?

I tilted my head and we moved into the lounge, full of old but comfortable furniture. I was proud of my home. It was small but it was paid for, despite the fact that I still continued to financially support my ex and the kids.

"Have a seat." I placed the beers and the bottle of wine onto the wooden coffee table, and then snapped my fingers. "Shit!"

I left the room again to grab a glass for Ash.

When I returned, the atmosphere had changed, even in that short space of time. It was now strained and fragile. Ash sat on the couch by herself, and Scott was in the armchair opposite.

Crap. You could cut the tension with a knife.

Time to grab the bull by the horns, so to speak. "Hey, bro. Can you move onto the couch with Ash? You're in my favorite chair."

He glared at me, and then stiffly got up and sat down on the couch next to Ash, but at the opposite end.

I swallowed a groan of frustration and took a sip of my beer as I collapsed into my comfortable recliner.

Ash turned to Scott, her hands folded elegantly in her lap. "So, Jack tells me your ex-wife is a real piece of work."

Pain shot through my throat as I choked on my beer. I coughed and spluttered but managed to get the alcohol down rather than breathe it in. Mostly.

Scott glared at me, the look one of surprise more than betrayal, before smiling grimly. Then he relaxed his posture and turned toward our outrageous woman.

"She is," he admitted with a shrug.

Ash moved closer to him, but they weren't touching. Not yet. "Is that why you've been reluctant to spend time with me and see if we're a perfect fit? Because you think I'll be like her?"

Fuck, our woman has balls.

She wasn't just outrageous; she was downright assertive when she wanted something. I needed to remember that for future reference.

I thumped myself on the chest to remove the remaining fluid from my lungs while Scott squirmed and cleared his throat. "Ah, yeah, I suppose. I hadn't really thought about it."

Ash narrowed her eyes. "Really?" Her tone said she didn't believe him.

Good girl. Keep going.

She was on a mission and obviously as impatient as I was. "You're kidding, right? We have the electricity thing, and you know I could be your perfect match, you're single, and you're not even curious to see if it's true?"

"If what's true?" Scott swallowed, his throat working hard.

"You're clearly intelligent, so don't disrespect the three of us by pretending you don't know."

Wow. Ash didn't miss a beat. "If the legends about perfect pairs are correct and that you and Jack are designed to love one woman."

Scott turned and gave me a look that said exactly what I was thinking. *Yeah, I know brother. She's gonna keep us on our toes.*

He nodded slowly.

I grinned at him and decided to try and help with the situation, if I could. "Sweetheart, could you give Scott a break for a minute? You know we've both spent our whole lives believing the legends were false. You've changed everything and we're trying to catch up."

Ash scowled at me. "Yeah, well two days ago I was sure I'd never find a man I could trust and that I was totally unlovable. But you changed all that, and I need to know if Scott is willing to give us a chance. I don't think I can survive being rejected again when I feel like I'm wide open."

Her voice wobbled at the end.

I grabbed my beer and tossed the rest of it back, feeling bad. I hadn't really thought about the risk to Ash herself.

I couldn't answer for Scott.

She was playing a dangerous game. If she pushed too hard, he could bolt.

I sat back and waited for him to respond.

He shifted and rubbed his hands over his pants like he was trying to wipe off sweat. "I can't guarantee anything, Ash, that's impossible."

My heart picked up pace and pounded against my rib cage. Would Scott be willing to try?

Ash took a deep breath and let it out in a sigh. "I know that, Scott, I really do, and if I thought for a moment that Jack and I could be happy as a couple, I'd leave you alone, I promise."

Whoa, she is walking a tightrope right now.

I rolled my empty beer glass between my palms, clenching my teeth to stop from blurting something out. My whole life and future happiness hung in the balance, and these two were talking it out in front of me like it wasn't the most important thing in the world.

Scott cleared his throat and asked the question that hung in the air. "You don't think you can be happy with just Jack?"

Ash shook her head. "No, I don't. Don't get me wrong." She shot a quick, slightly apologetic look my way. "Jack's awesome but when I saw my cousin at her wedding, I saw the balance her two men gave her. You offer things I need that Jack doesn't have. Just as he offers things you don't. A perfect pair sounds, well...perfect for a woman like me, and I believe Jack when he says that we need to be a family to be happy, but I...I won't force you. You need to want it too, otherwise..." She sighed heavily and my heart leapt, "I'll just go home at the end of the week and we can all go back to our old lives."

Hell, to the no! No way was I doing that.

Luckily, I realized that wouldn't be the smartest thing to say at this point and kept my mouth shut.

Scott glanced at me, then back to Ash, his brows high and his gaze thoughtful. "You mean what Laura, Tyler, and Brandon have. Yes?"

Ash jiggled where she sat, obviously working through her

nervous energy. "Yes! And I'm not asking for a commitment now. Hell, we don't know what's going to happen even tomorrow, but can you...maybe..."

She stopped and swallowed, and then looked at me. She'd run out of words, and I couldn't just sit and watch a minute longer.

I stood up and held out my hand, lifting Ash out of her seat. I guided her around the coffee table and to my side. "Scott, I know you're worried about shit we can't control, but I promise you that if you come and kiss her, touch her, it'll turn you into a believer."

I wrapped my arms around her waist from behind and stared at Scott over her head, silently begging with my eyes for him to understand. To give this a chance.

Scott stood up and scrubbed his face with his hands, and then rested both fists on his hips in a strange and uncomfortable way. "Okay, let's do this."

Hell yeah!

I nodded my head toward the hallway. "We may as well go into my bedroom. It's the biggest room and we can be comfortable."

It also had a king-sized bed, which I had bought out of sheer extravagance, but I was now glad I'd indulged.

I pulled Ash down the long hallway and into my large bedroom. We'd have to work out which house we wanted to live in long term, or whether we would buy something bigger for our new family.

But that was something to sort out later.

I stepped into my room and turned toward my mate.

My new life was finally beginning.

Scott

I STEPPED through Jack's bedroom door, ran my hand through my hair, and grabbed the back of my neck.

Now that I was here, I wasn't sure about this anymore. There were still so many variables in this relationship and far too many risk factors we hadn't considered.

I looked across the room and watched as Jack pulled Ash's dress over her head between kisses, the light material falling from his hands and pooling on the floor, her gorgeous body becoming visible for the first time.

Wow. She's gorgeous. All luscious curves and feminine beauty.

My breath hitched as Jack drew our mate into his arms, unclipped her bra at the back, and kissed her while the pale pink lace fell to the ground between them.

Lust slammed into me, knocking all caution and rational thought from my brain.

I needed her kisses too.

It had been so long since I'd been happy; since I'd felt the weight of depression lift. I could barely remember what it felt like, to be happy. If only for a moment, a night, I wanted to feel good again.

I pulled at the buttons on my shirt, discarding the clinging material and letting my breathing rate increase to match the thundering of my heart.

Jack and Ash looked toward me, a tangle of arms and golden skin.

Jack turned her in his arms so that she was facing me. I got a fleeting view of her large, soft breasts and pink nipples before he cupped them both and began kissing her neck.

A growl rose in my belly and I let the sound roll around the room as I strode forward, a burning need to claim this woman eating at me like a clawing hunger.

It's now or never.

I gripped her face with my hands and stared into her brilliant blue eyes for a single, heart-tugging moment before I brought my lips down on hers.

My whole body shuddered in pleasure at the first contact of her lips, and electrical sparks fired off into every cell of my starving body.

I groaned and hung onto her face as my grip on reality became more tenuous.

I swept my tongue into her mouth and the sweetness of her taste was overpowering.

Using every ounce of will power I possessed, I broke the connection and rested my forehead against hers.

I closed my eyes and muttered, "Oh, fuck."

Jack chuckled, and I looked up to see him grinning over Ash's shoulder. "That's only the half of it."

He let go of her bountiful breasts and slipped his hands down to her panties, bending to pull them down her long, shapely legs. She stepped out of the material, looking up at me with wide, scared eyes. She now stood before me completely naked.

I took a deep, shuddering breath that almost hurt as blood flowed south, hardening my cock and making my entire groin throb. I slid my hands down her warm arms, and then held her hands and took a step back, lifting her arms wide.

Her hands gripped mine hard, in obvious panic. *Is she shy? Why would she be shy? She is so beautiful.* I let a smile spread across my face as I drank her in. "You're magnificent."

And she was.

All woman.

Large, full breasts, a soft tummy, indented waist, and generously curved hips and thighs. She had a great figure and looked strong— every inch the Amazon needed to take on both Jack and me.

I let my wandering gaze lift back up to her gorgeous face. She bit her lip, looking terribly nervous.

"I cannot wait to taste every inch of you, Ashleigh," I said.

Her hands slipped from mine and she crossed her arms to cover herself.

That won't do.

"Don't do that. You're absolutely perfect." I stepped forward and kissed her, shuddering softly as her warm, soft breasts connected with my chest and her fingers moved up to thread into my hair. I feasted on her lips, letting my hands roam all over her luscious body —squeezing her hips, spanning her trim waist, teasing the crack of her ass, and following the curve of her spine. She was all hot skin and softness, incredible beneath my palms and fingertips.

She moaned into my mouth, so I slipped my hand between her legs, feeling her shiver and open. I teased her soft flesh with my fingertips, groaning as I passed over her slippery lips and already swollen clit.

She gasped and pressed closer. I turned my hand around, flicking her clit with my thumb and sliding my middle finger into her wet pussy.

"Oh, Scott!" Her head fell back as I worked her flesh.

My name on her lips was so hot my cock thickened to an almost painful width. Her nails dug into my bare shoulders, her breath coming in delightful pants and gasps.

She was truly magnificent to watch, her skin flushed and her eyes closed in pleasure as I pushed her toward climax.

I forced my eyes to stay open, not wanting to miss a moment of the first time I made my mate come.

She sagged against me as her knees weakened and her back bowed. She was so close.

"Come for me, sweetheart, please," I said in a low, husky voice. "I need to feel you come apart for me."

She cried out and clung to me as her body tightened and began to spasm, her pussy clenching around my fingers in rippling waves.

Heat passed over me, pride flaring in my chest as she shook in my arms.

When she finally went limp and I withdrew my hand, I held her while she trembled.

This is it. What I've been aching for.

Something warm and soothing slid over my heart, healing old but still open wounds that I'd clung to for years. This was what lovemaking was meant to feel like, and I hadn't even gotten her into the bed yet.

Hell, I was still half dressed!

"Bring her over here."

I looked up, somehow surprised to hear another voice in the room. Jack had stripped completely and motioned at the bed where he'd pulled back the sheets.

"Lay her down in the center of the mattress," he said.

Ash swayed toward the sound of his voice, and I guided her to the bed and helped her to lie down.

"I'm having her first," he said.

I clenched my teeth as I unclasped my belt and pushed my trousers down my thighs.

My cock bounced out against my belly, hot and aching.

No problems getting hard tonight.

"And why's that?" I asked.

Jack narrowed his eyes at me as he ripped open a condom and rolled it on. "Because I've been waiting too fucking long. We've both been waiting for you."

"You mean you haven't...?"

Shock passed through me. Did Jack seriously expect me to believe he hadn't fucked her yet?

"Yes, I mean we didn't have sex last night," he said. "Or this morning."

"Why?"

He groaned in frustration. "Because it didn't feel right without you!"

I glanced down at Ash for clarification and she shook her head slowly.

Wow. I had no idea...

Jack pointed at me. "So, I'm going first, okay? And besides, her mouth is fucking divine. Go try it."

Ash moaned from the bed as she cupped her breasts and tweaked her own nipples. "That was so beautiful, Scott, thank you."

I smiled at her, feeling an uncomfortable squeeze around my heart.

God, she's beautiful.

Jack climbed onto the bed and slid between her spread thighs.

What the fuck am I waiting for!

I crawled onto the bed, and she wrapped her legs around Jack. He surged forward and they both cried out as they joined for the first time.

A bolt of pleasure hit me right in the gut and precum wept from the head of my cock as Jack took her with measured strokes. I'd never seen anything more erotic, which was hard to admit. I couldn't believe the hottest thing I'd ever witnessed was my brother taking our woman.

But it was Ash that made it hot. So fucking hot, seeing the desire in her half-closed eyes and hearing her little murmurs of enjoyment.

I wrapped my hand around my cock and squeezed hard. I wanted to come right there. My balls were aching, the tip of my cock was deep red, and what I was watching was so fucking hot I just wanted to squirt all over her.

Jack came off her body, pulled her to the edge of the bed, and dove back into her wet pussy.

She cried out and I squeezed harder.

Fuck me...

Jack grunted. "Beautiful girl, give Scott your mouth if you can."

She turned her gaze toward me. "Oh, I'd love to. Come here, sweetie."

She motioned with her hands and I took a breath.

Could I do this?

Yes!

I crawled forward, lined up my cock with her open lips, and watched with fascination as the intelligent, beautiful woman of my dreams took me into her mouth.

Wet, hot, exquisite pressure wrapped around the head of my cock.

I pulled out, trying to slow down.

She looked at me, a gasp and a moan escaping her lips as Jack continued to move within her. "What's wrong?"

I grinned and guided my cock back to her mouth. "I almost came right then. Your mouth feels incredible."

She smiled up at me as I slid back into her mouth, and Jack began to move again. She moaned and sucked harder.

Oh, fuck!

My eyes shut as I threw my head back and growled, flexing my hips and thrusting in time with her bobbing head. She hummed around my cock as Jack fucked her harder and faster.

The heat was unbearable and so delicious I couldn't stand it. Prickles danced up my thighs just as she pulled off my cock and began to scream.

Jack fell forward onto her body as I pulled away, capturing her freed mouth in a kiss as he thrust deep, groaning loudly as they shuddered together.

Long moments passed in the heated room and I began to cool down, my control in place and my body aching.

My heart wasn't that far behind. Fuck, second again to my perfect, footballer brother.

Maybe I should leave?

I couldn't stand being pushed aside and rejected. Yet again.

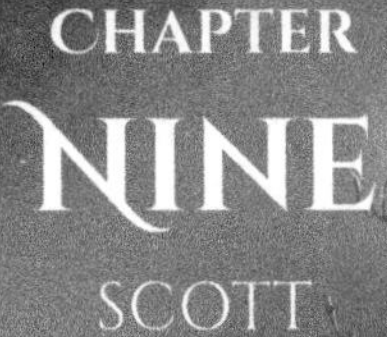

CHAPTER
NINE

SCOTT

My chest burned as Jack rolled off Ash's sweaty body and he kissed her on the forehead.

"I'll be right back." He got up and moved to the bathroom to dispose of the condom.

I slid off the bed, acid in my gut making me want to throw up as I headed to the door. What the hell else had I expected? Something balanced?

Ridiculous.

"Hey!"

I turned at the sound of Ash's voice as she slipped off the bed and walked over to me, her gorgeous breasts bouncing as she walked. "What happened? Don't you want me anymore?"

She stood in front of me, naked, frowning, and smelling of sex and sweat.

Of course, I bloody well wanted her! "Yeah, but you pushed me away so you could make love to Jack, so I just assumed we were done..."

Her mouth dropped open.

Had I got that wrong?

"Pushed you away? No, I had to let go of you or I would have bitten you when I came. I didn't mean to push you away. Not at all."

Some of the disappointment disappeared from my gut. She was right. How could she have stayed in that one position the whole time?

"Sorry," I muttered. "I'm not used to this dynamic."

She put her hands on her hips. "Well, neither am I. But I'm a fast learner."

She dropped to her knees on the carpet and took my semi-erect cock back into her mouth, using her hands and lips to work me hard and fast.

The heat and suction almost brought me to my knees as the world whirled around me in swirling lights.

Everything came to me at once as my logic clicked into place.

She didn't reject me. Not at all.

"Oh, God!" I slid my hand into her hair, holding her skull as she moved up and down on me. It would take time to become accustomed to our three-way lovemaking, but as long as Ash wanted me too, I'd learn to cope.

Yeah, and next time, I'll take her first.

Heat tickled my lower spine and I pulled her off me with a fast twist of my hips. "Enough. On the bed. On your knees."

Was that my voice? I sounded like I'd busted my windpipe and could only talk from my lowest octave.

Ash squealed like an excited little girl, ran, and jumped up on the bed, kneeling on the mattress and then going down onto all fours.

Lust kicked me in the gut.

"Ashleigh, you are seriously, absolutely, beautiful." I walked up behind her and pressed down on her lower back, gasping when her pink, slick folds came into view.

"Here." Jack appeared from somewhere and pressed a condom into my hand. I blindly opened it and slid it on with difficulty. When was the last time I'd done any of this?

Jack moved onto the bed and lay perpendicular to us, kissing Ash and touching her face and back.

I looked down at her body and licked my lips. I had to have a taste. Just for a minute.

I grabbed a handful of flesh on either side of her gorgeous ass, opened her up, and licked the swollen, red flesh from clit to ass.

She screamed and pushed back toward me. My head swam as the most delicious flavors I'd ever tasted burst across my tongue.

I pressed my tongue deeply inside her, licking and eating at her until she was crying out.

The scent of her was divine; I could lap at her cream all day.

I continued to follow the curves and shapes of her pink flesh with my tongue until her gasps became frantic.

"Scott!" she gasped. "Please!"

I straightened up, grabbed her hips, and thrust in to the hilt in one slide.

She started to come around my cock, crying out out and pushing back, the ripples of her pussy dragging on me in the most seductive way.

No, I can't... Not already.

Heat licked at my balls, and that uncontrollable tingle made its way through my body. I was going to come. I couldn't stop it now.

I groaned and Ash grabbed at my hand where I gripped her hips, making a connection, giving me something extra to hold onto.

My balls pulsed and my orgasm swept me away. Lights exploded in my head as my seed squirted into the condom.

Ash relaxed beneath my hands as her orgasm receded and I withdrew from her body, self-disappointment sucking at me with poisonous talons.

What a despicable performance. She'll hate me for sure, now.

Ash fell onto her tummy, and then moaned and stretched, rolling over to look up at me. "You coming here to cuddle?"

She held her arms up and gave me a blissful smile.

"Ah, yeah. Give me a sec." I moved away to the ensuite and

cleaned up, and then walked back into the bedroom with a lethargy that made all my muscles heavy and dragging.

Jack was already laying on the bed, cuddled in behind Ashleigh.

I pulled up all of my mental walls, fully expecting to be shunned after what had just happened. I'd come in seconds. My ex-wife would have just about punched me in the face for such a disgraceful act.

I glanced at my clothes that lay on the floor. Perhaps I should head home and sleep in my own bed tonight.

"Get in the bed, you idiot," Jack said, as if he could sense my intent.

I sighed. He was right. I *was* being an idiot.

I slipped beneath the covers, turning my back on the other two. I'd never slept with three people in a bed, but for tonight, I'd try.

Ash's warm hand moved over my waist and around my middle, then pulled on my chest, hard. I resisted the pull and closed my eyes, pretending to sleep.

"Scott, honey? Can you lie on your back for a minute?"

I let a sigh escape and rolled onto my back, pulling the blankets up to my chin.

Here we go.

I forced my eyes open and turned my head toward her, waiting for the chastisement.

She was smiling and moved closer to lay her hand across my chest, and then pressed her lips against my shoulder. The heat of her was so tempting, but I dare not cuddle into her.

"Thank you so much, that was incredible," she said.

I stared at her, shocked. "What are you talking about? I came after only one thrust."

She giggled and kissed my shoulder again. "You mean after you already made me cum with your hands? Then I sucked you for ages, you licked me until I was right on the edge, and then I had such a massive orgasm I dragged you with me? How awesome is that? Never be sorry for being in sync with me. That's a huge compliment!"

You've got to be kidding me.

I couldn't believe her. She simply couldn't be that...*nice.*

"Come here, beautiful." Jack pulled her back against him and spooned her, but she kept her hand on me.

My gut churned but I stayed where I was.

"Can you turn onto your side so I can touch you?" she asked.

I lay there for a moment, hot tears stinging my eyes.

My thoughts were tumbling around so much my head ached. Why would she want to cuddle? Was she serious about actually being happy with our lovemaking?

When she continued to smile and run her hands over my arm, I had to assume she was at least partly telling the truth.

I slowly rolled onto my side, facing away from her, and shuffled back until I could feel the heat of her body against my back.

Her palm slipped over my hip, and her soft sigh sounded happy. "Goodnight."

Her whispered word made me smile, and the black cloud hanging over me finally began to lift.

I was an insomniac; had been since my marriage had started to fail, so I didn't have much hope of getting any real rest.

But despite my misgivings, the night was magical. Just to lay there, with someone touching me, and feel wanted, not rejected. That was new.

I didn't even mind that I would be awake while they slept. That just meant I would have more time to enjoy it.

Through the dark hours, Ash stayed close and often nestled into me in her sleep.

I finally fell asleep around three a.m. and when I awoke in the morning, she was kissing my back in gentle, soft touches.

In that moment, I knew my life had changed.

Now to see if it would last.

CHAPTER
TEN

ASH

We were in Jack's kitchen and the morning light filtered in through the front windows.

Scott was dressed, and ready for a day he had planned with his kids. Jack had told me the relationship between Scott and his offspring was strained, and the last thing he should do was cancel on them last minute.

"I really don't want to leave, Ash. I'm so sorry."

The regret in Scott's voice was heart-warming, his words obviously sincere. I smiled at him and stepped forward, wrapping my arms around his neck to stare up into his handsome face.

His green eyes were wary at first, and then the look melted away as he let his hands settle on my hips. He tugged me close.

It was truly beautiful to watch him let down his guard, bit by bit. His whole body relaxed as though I'd pulled the pin on the tension surrounding him, and he leaned into my embrace.

Thank goodness for that.

I smiled up at him. "I know, but I respect the fact that you have to."

And I did.

Not that I ever thought I'd date anyone who had kids, but I loved the fact that Scott took his responsibilities seriously and hadn't allowed my presence to derail plans he'd already made with his children. "How many kids do you have?"

He smiled softly. "Three. Meaghan's eighteen, Tommy's sixteen, and Ryan is fifteen."

I whistled softly. "That's close together."

He shrugged. "Suppose so."

He hummed gently as he moved closer and rubbed his nose against mine, the gesture speaking volumes about his need for touch.

I lifted my hands so that I could touch his face, and he jerked back as if expecting a smack. *Oh, sweetheart.*

I looked him in the eyes. "I will never hurt you, Scott."

Never. Especially not physically.

His green eyes went wide and I couldn't resist leaning forward and pressing my lips to his, the sweetest moan reaching my ears from his throat as I shifted closer.

Why would someone, especially a woman who professed to love him—the mother of his *children*, no less—hurt a man like this? Why would anyone deliberately hurt *anyone*?

"You two starting without me?" The joking tone broke through our intense moment, but I didn't mind. Jack would hopefully balance us out and stop Scott and I from being too serious all the time.

I turned so I could look at Jack who was walking into the kitchen, but stayed close to Scott, pressing my body against my sweet, complex man. The soft touch of his lips against my hair made me sigh and snuggle closer.

I'd never get sick of this type of affection. Hopefully, if there were *two* of them to give and receive cuddles and kisses, the touching and love wouldn't disappear like it had from my first marriage.

"No, just saying goodbye," I said.

Jack nodded and reached out for me, a look of hunger in his blue eyes.

Really? You want to cuddle, too?

More than a little amused at their need to be holding me all the time, I put my hand in Jack's and he pulled me away from Scott. I let a laugh fill the space around us. When was the last time I'd felt this happy?

Easy answer: Never!

Jack twirled me around so my back was against his chest and his arms went around my waist, holding me tight. I relaxed instantly.

There was something comforting about having such a big, strong male holding me. I felt so safe.

"You got kid shit to do?" Jack asked his brother, and I smiled to myself.

Lovely language, Mr. Football.

Scott nodded, scraping his keys noisily along the kitchen bench before palming them. "Yeah, gotta see Meaghan for lunch, but I'll be back later. You guys going to be here?"

I glanced up as Jack looked down, his eyebrows raised in question.

I shrugged. "I haven't got any plans other than being here with you."

Although I did need to work out what on earth I was going to do at the end of the week when I was meant to go home and resume my life.

Both men purred like sated cats and I glanced up in alarm. That wasn't the first time I'd heard them make that particular sound. "What the hell is that noise you guys do?"

The happy sound stopped like a switch had been thrown.

Jack squeezed me tight and kissed the top of my head. "We'll explain it to you later. One shock at a time, I think."

Scott nodded. "I agree, and I better run. See you guys later."

I frowned but waved at Scott as he headed out the door.

I didn't like them avoiding a question I was pretty sure was going to lead to something important.

But I would let the men distract me, because if they didn't tell me soon, I'd just ask my cousin. Laura would make sure I knew everything I needed to, anyway.

"So, what are we doing today, beautiful girl?"

I leaned into Jack's strength and wiggled my ass against the rising hardness pressing against me.

My body ached from the night before, but there was a hunger that was rising once again within me that I was beginning to recognize.

"Bed, maybe?" I said as I wiggled again.

I released a happy squeal as my feet left the ground and I was unceremoniously carried back to our room of pleasure.

WHILE SCOTT WAS out with his kids, I stayed at Jack's house. After we'd made love once again, I got up, had a shower, and enjoyed the feeling of my happy mood infiltrating my whole being.

The music inside my head swayed my whole body, making my hips swing from side to side. I hummed a little and smiled to myself. Maybe I could make us some dinner? What did Jack eat, other than steak?

"You sound happy, beautiful girl."

Jack's deep voice slid into my ear as his arms embraced me in their strength and warmth. Fresh, spicy scents filled my nostrils. He smelled great with or without a shower.

"Hmm, I am happy."

How could I not be?

My body was still singing from the multiple orgasms I'd had in the past twenty-four hours, and it looked like my beautiful, damaged Scott wanted to love me, too.

Which was amazing!

It seemed ridiculous that my life had taken such a massive shift from where it had been only a week ago. But I was going with it. I wiped down the clean kitchen counter top for the second time, feeling the need to nest already. I could do so much with this house.

"Hey, Jack—" I opened my mouth to ask him about the boundaries of his property, when a loud commotion outside the house reached my ears.

I frowned and turned toward the sound.

What the hell is that?

The back door burst open and a red-faced teenager huffed her way into the room, followed closely by Scott, whose mouth was twisted into a frowny grimace.

"*Her?*" The girl pointed at me. "You cannot be serious, Dad!"

I blinked at the girl. She was obviously his oldest daughter. She had his gorgeous green eyes, square jaw, and flowing brown hair.

Scott grabbed for his daughter's arm. "Meaghan, stop being so rude!"

Meaghan stamped her foot on the tiled floor like a toddler. "She's not even a shifter! How can you guys be so stupid?"

A shifter? What the hell was a shifter?

Meaghan growled and stomped her foot again.

Okay, so maybe she looked like her dad, but from the little I'd heard about the girl's mother, she obviously had a temperament like her mom.

Jack growled in return and stepped closer to her, the tension in the room painfully high as the three family members postured and snarled at each other.

That was just *weird*.

Meaghan turned back toward Scott. "You're supposed to be with Mom! You never even worked on it. You can't just give up on your marriage."

Scott groaned and threw his hands up in the air. "Meaghan, I worked on it for twenty years! Twenty years! I know you don't even have a concept of how much time that is—but I did *everything* I knew how to do to keep us all together. There was nothing left for me to do."

Meaghan growled again, louder and deeper this time, and when she spoke, her words were garbled. "No. It's *her* fault. She broke up our family. You would have come back to Mom if it wasn't for her."

Horror struck me across the chest. Was that true? It couldn't be! I couldn't be responsible for breaking up a family!

Scott shook his head and crossed his arms over his chest. "Meaghan, the marriage ended five years ago, and you know it never really should have begun. Your mom and I never suited each other."

Meaghan growled in an inhuman way. "That's not true!"

My heart jumped in my chest as Meaghan began to change before my eyes.

Her body grew more hair and her face transformed into an ugly, grotesque mask. Then the pretty teenage girl was gone, and a small cougar stood in her place.

What. The. Fuck.

"Oh, my God!" I screamed and jumped back as the animal surged toward me.

Then my men disappeared in the same way, and suddenly there were two more, very large, cinnamon-colored big cats circling each other, growling and hissing.

No fucking way!

I inched back and hopped up onto the kitchen counter, lifting my legs and curling up into a ball. A thin film of sweat coated my body, and I slipped against the stone counter as I trembled.

My heart was racing, yet I couldn't move. Now that I was up here, I was frozen in place.

"Impossible. This is not happening." I could barely get the words out as every muscle in my body locked down.

The smaller cat, obviously Meaghan, was being herded toward the door by the two larger cats. Then, suddenly she was practically pushed out the door into the backyard and they all took off into the forest behind the house.

I forced my legs to uncurl and allowed my feet to touch the ground. I needed to get out of here *right fucking now.*

The keys to Jack's truck sat on a coffee table nearby and I grabbed them before stumbling out the door.

I tried to breathe, but my chest ached too much. In the distance, feral catlike noises sounded and my already fast heart rate began to thunder.

"I've... I've gotta get out of here..." I muttered.

I jumped into his truck, threw it into gear, and drove blindly away from the house, my mind in utter chaos.

"What the fuck...What the fuck..." I continued to chant as I drove, scanning the deserted roads. When I finally felt like I was far enough from the crazy scene, I stopped at a cross road.

What the hell should I do? Where should I go? *Ohmygod...* My body was ice cold, but my frazzled brain stopped whirling long enough to focus on a single line of thought.

Laura.

I took out my cell phone and dialled her number, praying to whatever being watched over me in this life.

Please, let her answer!

"Ashleigh! How are you, honey?" Laura's upbeat voice was the best sound I'd ever heard, and a small sob escaped my throat.

"Laura," I said, trying to keep calm. "Are you home yet?"

There was silence for a moment, and I realized my panic might not have been as deeply buried as I thought.

"Ah, yeah, we got in an hour ago," she began. "Honey, what's wrong?"

My two boyfriends just turned into fucking mountain lions and ran off. I let out a sob before I could stop myself.

"Can I come stay with you tonight? I don't want to crash the honeymoon or anything, just... *please...*"

Oh shit, I was being so selfish! My cousin had just gotten

married, for goodness' sake! Hot, salty tears leaked down my face, and a large lump rose in my throat like a tidal wave.

What was the other alternative? The airport?

Leave Scott and Jack, and never look back?

I bit down on my lip and held my breath, yet another sob escaped.

Laura jumped in. "Of course, Ash! Come over, but sweetie… what's happened?"

I fumbled around the cabin for a tissue box, took some deep breaths, and focused on speaking.

"I'm…going to…drive over," I said between breaths. "Then tell you. Okay?"

"Of course, Ash, but please be careful. We're not going anywhere. You take as long as you need."

I made a humming noise in my throat and hung up before I embarrassed myself even more.

I put the phone down and let my head fall back against the headrest. My chest hurt, my eyes stung, and I couldn't get enough air into my lungs.

Finally, I let go of all control and let the angry, hurt, confused tears come.

So much had happened in such a short amount of time, and those animals…

I shuddered. It was all just…too much.

Eventually, the retching sobs slowed and I regained a small amount of control over my mind and body.

I blew out a long breath and pushed the hair out of my eyes. Time to see how much damage I'd done. I looked in the mirror and grimaced at my reflection.

I was bright red, from the tip of my nose to my once-white eyeballs.

"Oh, shit," I muttered.

I looked as bad as I felt. I was exhausted, my entire body aching from both the crying and now the adrenaline crash.

I huffed and sat up straight in the car seat.

"Okay, Laura's house."

I pressed buttons on my cell phone, put the location of Laura's new home into the navigator, and slid the truck's stick into drive.

It was time to find out exactly what I was dealing with.

ELEVEN

After we'd gotten my feral teenage daughter back to my house to change into some clean clothes, I'd turned tail and raced straight back to Jack's house.

I shifted in the back yard, and heedless of my state of undress, ran straight into the house. My muscles trembled with the amount of adrenaline pumping through my blood stream, but I needed to find Ash.

Guilt and anger threaded through my gut. I should never have tried to talk to Meaghan about Ashleigh. *Fucking teenagers!* All rampant hormones and no bloody sense! Couldn't control themselves if their lives depended on it. Her lion had come out due to anger and stress.

She was still quite young as far as shifters go, since we only began changing once we hit puberty.

Yeah, well, what was your excuse?

I grimaced. Jack and I hadn't been much better than my teenage daughter, losing our temper like we had. We should have stayed calm, at least one of us, and talked Ash through the ordeal.

When Meaghan had shifted, our need to protect our mate had

overruled all common sense and the next thing I knew, all three of us had been in lion form.

And if I was honest, pure frustration and anger at the situation had probably been a driving force in my shift too.

I swallowed hard and focused on the job at hand: finding my mate and reassuring her that everything was okay.

"Ashleigh? You here, honey?" I called.

I walked through Jack's house, checking the living areas, bedrooms, and even the bathroom. Nothing.

"Hey, Scott. Is she here?" Jack's voice bellowed through the walls from the kitchen.

The hairs on my body prickled up, a fine shiver coursing down my spine.

"No, she's gone." I walked back into the kitchen and faced my brother, who was panting from the run back to the house and covered in sweat.

"She'll be back at the hotel, then," he said. "Let's grab some clothes and go."

Jack started picking up his clothing off the floor of the kitchen where it had fallen earlier and quickly dressed. I did the same. Then I leaned back against the kitchen counter, my knees weakening at the idea of never seeing Ashleigh again.

"What if she's not at the hotel, Jack? What if she took off some place?"

Jack shrugged as though he was indifferent, but the set of his jaw belied his casual shrug. "Then we'll find her, even if we have to drive to Toronto and drag her back here."

My knees were seriously not going to hold my weight any longer. I lunged for a kitchen chair and grabbed the back of it. I managed to swing it around and plant my ass on the hard seat before my legs gave out.

"Ah..." I massaged my thighs as my mind whirled with the implications of her disappearance.

I couldn't believe my brother was being so naïve. How was that possible after the life we'd lived? We could probably track Ash down, since we knew where she worked and lived, but what would we do with her then?

She'd just witnessed us shift into mountain lions. I couldn't imagine how a non-shifter would process that information if they hadn't known about it beforehand.

"And if she doesn't want us anymore?" I said. "If she's too freaked out by the fact that we shift into fucking animals? What then?"

Jack growled, his eyes flashing gold as his lion rose to the surface. Then he began to pace, the floor beneath his feet creaking with strain.

"She has to—she's ours!"

I let my head drop into my hands, fear filling me up like an infection, spreading through my body and overcoming all the good that Ashleigh had done earlier.

I'd known something like this would happen. The promise of paradise I'd seen in her eyes and felt in her touches last night had been too good to be true.

I let the cold pain consume me and clenched my teeth until my jaw cracked.

I sat in my chair and clung to the promise of oblivion that was on its way. I knew this feeling only too well. What an idiot to believe I had any hope of paradise.

Ash

I PULLED up outside a beautiful house with a winding path, which sat in the most magnificent position beneath the mountains.

The front door was carved and as I squinted at it to see the image properly, I realized with a shock that it looked like a mountain lion.

Holy hell!

I began to hyperventilate, panic constricting my throat and lungs. I'd seen the same door at Laura's wedding. Brandon and Tyler's parents had a similar entrance to their grand home.

My breath wheezed in and out between my lips and I gripped the steering wheel harder. My head felt light, black spots spinning around my line of sight.

They were *all* lions? *Oh, my God...*

Laura's voice came barrelling into my space. "What the hell! Ashleigh?"

The truck door opened, and I inhaled, my ribs aching with dull pain. The air was cold as it entered, and my teeth chattered.

I exhaled and my breath shuddered. I needed air so badly, and a part of my brain told me that I was overreacting, yet...I couldn't stop it. My stomach clenched with a wave of nausea.

"Sweetheart, stop panicking, breathe slowly." Laura knelt down on the grass next to my car and pressed her hands into my thighs. The pressure was something to cling to, and I focused on her stare.

"It's okay," she said. "I'm here. Breathe."

I closed my eyes, tears slipping down my cheeks. I ignored them as I focused on breathing.

In—oh, that hurts—and out. That's a bit better.

I repeated the words over and over, listening to Laura's soothing voice until I could breathe almost normally.

When I finally opened my eyes, I let my hands slip from the steering wheel and into my lap, my shoulders sagging in pain and exhaustion.

"Come inside," she said, standing.

A sob escaped my throat and I wiped at my eyes with my palms. Everything hurt so much.

Laura all but dragged me from the car, and I moved in a daze toward the house. There were no more words spoken.

I was led into a bedroom, my body moving on auto-pilot, but eventually I lay on a soft bed. Muffled male voices carried from somewhere in the house. Laura's men? My men? I didn't care.

I didn't want to see them.

No men, no strangers, no *shifters*.

A gentle hand touched my forehead and I curled up on my side, sighing as a warm cotton blanket was pulled up over me, creating a cocoon of heat.

"Sleep, sweetheart," Laura whispered.

I nodded and let the blackness consume me.

I OPENED my eyes and stretched out my aching legs, a welcome relief as the muscles lengthened and popped.

God, that's better.

I blinked several times and rolled onto my back, stretching again. The room Laura had put me in was lovely, with textured paint on the feature wall behind me.

I sat up slowly and looked around for the first time. My head throbbed from all the crying and my eyes felt like they'd been rubbed raw with sandpaper.

But my head was clear, and I could breathe.

I was in a bedroom, obviously set up for guests. It was free of photos and personal trinkets, yet the soft colors and homely bed cover made it comfortable and cozy.

There was even an ensuite bathroom.

I groaned as I twisted and swung my legs off the bed. The world wasn't quite steady yet. I stood up and waited a moment while my head spun and my stomach tightened, in need of nourishment.

"I take it back," I said to myself. "I feel like crap."

It was the understatement of the century, but it made me feel better to say something out loud.

I pushed myself to walk to the bathroom and splashed some cold water on my sore eyes. I gasped as the icy water touched my skin, then let it slide over my lips and into my mouth, swallowing some.

My belly gurgled as I stood up and stared into the mirror.

My cheeks were flushed, my eyes were red and bulging, and my hair was just about sticking up on end.

I splashed more water onto my face and patted down my skin with a hand towel that lay next to the sink. Then I ran my hands through my hair, attempting to straighten it out.

My stomach jumped again and I placed a hand over my belly, trying to quiet the nerves. I needed to relax. I'd come here for help, and I was sure I'd find it.

I checked my reflection once more before I left the bedroom, opened the door, and crept along the hallway toward the sound of voices.

I was almost at the end of the corridor when a rather sexy male voice came from the kitchen. "Are you going to get her up soon, Laura?"

I halted and listened. They were talking about me.

"Maybe," Laura said. "It's getting dark and she might be hungry."

As though on cue my tummy gurgled so loudly I was sure they would have heard it.

I gathered my courage and stepped into the modern, brightly lit kitchen. "Yeah, I kinda am."

My heart thumped against my ribs as Laura, Tyler, and Brandon turned to look at me. The men jumped up and I stepped back, the testosterone and energy in the room feeling the same way it had with Jack and Scott before they'd turned into lions.

I pushed out with both hands, as though I could stop them. "No! Don't do it! Please."

Laura jumped up from her kitchen stool and put both her hands out. "It's okay, it's okay. Tyler and Brandon won't hurt you, honey. They're just big. Sit down, boys. Please."

There was a moment of silence in which all the air from my lungs left me and a squeezing sensation wrapped around my ribcage. I didn't want to see lions again.

I *really* didn't.

Brandon and Tyler both sat back down, and I sucked in some much-needed oxygen, as the atmosphere in the room calmed.

Laura moved forward and gestured to the stool on her side of the island bench. "Sit down here, sweetie. I'll make you something to eat. Do you want a sandwich, or there's left over chicken stir-fry?"

My stomach growled and I giggled nervously. "I'd love some stir-fry, Laura. Thanks."

I needed something to drink, too.

Tyler, the dark-haired husband, silently wandered over to a fridge and took out a few bottles. Without speaking, he placed them on the table in front of me and took out a couple of glasses from the cupboard. He lifted his gaze to me once he'd backed away and sat in his chair once again.

I swallowed the lump that rose in my throat. Why had I been so afraid of these men? They were obviously kind and loving; I'd seen it at their wedding.

"Thanks, Tyler," I said, voice hoarse

I took the bottle of apple juice with two hands, opened it, and poured some into a glass without spilling any. Which was impressive, considering the amount of shaking my hands were doing.

Laura placed a bowl of hot food in front of me and I picked up the fork and ate. The chicken had a beautiful honey soy marinade on it, and I ate most of it without lifting my head. Once my tummy was happy, I looked up to see my cousin staring at me with those assessing green eyes of hers.

"What?" I asked, holding my fork over my bowl.

Laura burst out laughing, and then slapped her hand on the table. "What? What do you mean, 'what'! What the fuck happened?"

"Did you just...?" I couldn't help it. I laughed, lowering my fork.

Had my very proper cousin, the talented Dr. Laura, just said "fuck"?

She grinned at me, her understanding obvious. "Yeah well, some situations call for that word."

The hysteria dissipated, and I wiped away the tears that had gathered. "That was just too funny."

"Yeah, yeah, don't change the topic. What happened since our wedding? The last thing I knew, Jack and Scott were sniffing around you, looking very much like another perfect pair who had found their mate, and now you're here in tears. Having stolen Jack's truck, I might add! So, I'm guessing that would be 'cause you saw them in lion form, yeah?"

Laura's summation was like a bucket of cold water, sobering me instantly. "How did you...? Yeah, that's about right."

The men moved, slowly, as though I'd bolt like a frightened animal, and pulled up stools next to Laura at the kitchen counter.

Brandon spoke first, his muscles a little too like Jack's for my mental health.

God, I miss him already.

Brandon's lips turned up at the corners as he said, "They obviously screwed it up. Even Laura didn't bolt the first time she saw us shift."

I huffed out a little laugh. "Yeah, well, I'm sure she had some warning. I knew something was up with the whole perfect pair thing, but animals? For goodness' sake!"

Tyler poured more juice into my empty glass and smiled kindly. "What happened, exactly? Can you start from after the wedding?"

They'd missed so much.

I sighed and let my shoulders sag. I didn't really want to regale them with the whole scenario, but I had come here for help, so...

"Well, Jack took me home after the wedding and pretty much told me I'm their chosen mate and—oh, shit! Now that makes sense—I never got the whole *mate* thing. Weird word to use. Anyway, we spent some time together and despite all my hang-ups about men, Jack somehow managed to convince me that we were perfect together."

It all seemed so stupid now.

Laura smiled at me and glanced at both her men. "Of course, he did because you are, honey. Did you get the electrical zap thing when you touched them?"

"How did you...?" I glanced between the trio and shrugged. "Of course. It's one of the signs, isn't it?"

Laura nodded with a grin on her pretty face. "Yes, as well as feeling completely safe and happy while you're with them. Between the two of them, their personalities match every list you ever made about your perfect man, don't they?"

I smiled a little, stinging hot tears gathering once again in my eyes. "Yeah, they do. I always knew you couldn't get a guy that was relaxed, yet serious, smart yet crass, super funny and super intelligent."

Brandon and Tyler laughed and high-fived behind their wife's back.

Brandon puffed up his chest as he spoke. "Did she just describe us as her perfect men?"

I shook my head at them while they covered Laura in kisses. "Stop, both of you. We need to fix this."

The guys grinned and returned to their seats.

Laura fixed me with a stare. "What's the actual problem? I know it's freaky, but it's just a genetic thing, like having blue eyes. They have full control over everything. They'd never hurt you."

I wasn't so sure about that teenage daughter of Scott's, but really, Meaghan was the least of my worries. I looked away and down, picking at my nails and trying hard to focus on something that I actually understood.

"Ashleigh!" Laura said.

"What?" I looked up to see her glaring at me. "I don't know, Laura, I don't. Number one, it isn't just freaky. It's bloody, amazingly, out of this world. I'm still trying to wrap my head around it."

Tyler sat forward a bit. "What did Jack and Scott say?"

I shrugged. "I haven't spoken to them. Scott and his daughter ran into the kitchen and started fighting, and then all three of them transformed into snarling mountain lions and ran out of the house and off into the forest. I haven't spoken to them since."

Tyler's eyes bulged. "So, you haven't even talked to them about all this? Shit, no wonder you ran."

The three of them shared understanding looks which made me feel better.

Maybe I should have stuck around to ask questions, but I didn't have a choice once the anxiety attack set in.

Brandon *tsked* loudly. "Well, Laura pretty much summed it up. We're born with the ability to shift at any time, and it kicks in around puberty. Our whole family does it. You can't catch it, so don't worry. We have full control in our animal form and would definitely not harm anyone, especially not our mate."

My head began to ache, and my brain was definitely overloaded. "I think I might go lie down again."

I slid off the seat, a weird sort of numbness slipping over me. "Is that okay?"

Laura jumped off her chair and walked back around the counter, taking my hand in hers. "Of course, it is. Let's go."

We walked down the long hallway to the guestroom, and I made my way to the bed. I climbed onto the comfortable mattress, pulling up the blankets. My eyes were heavy, and everything was too hard at the moment. I needed sleep. Everything would make more sense in the morning.

I hoped.

"You know they love you already, Ash," Laura said from the doorway. "No matter what else is going through your head, you need to know that those men would have fallen in love with you from the moment you touched. Nothing will keep them from working everything out with you. If you want that, too."

I forced my lids open, hot tears gathering at the back of my eyes. "I'm not sure I want to work things out, Laura. The shifting thing is scary, but that can obviously be overcome. You accepted it. There's more to it than that."

I took a steadying breath and spoke the words I'd been terrified to even think about. "Scott's so broken, and his daughter is horrible. I don't know if I can join a family with so much pain already in it."

My voice caught on the words. Taking on a man who already had children had always been something I swore I'd never do.

Let alone *two men*, both with children to other women.

I'd already escaped a bad marriage and poisonous environment. I didn't want to join another one.

Laura gave me a reassuring smile. "I'm sure there's a way for you all to work things out, Ash. Please don't give up on them. These men are a dream come true. You have no idea."

I let my eyes drop down, shutting out the light and my optimistic cousin.

"Night, Laura."

As much as I wanted to stay, I wasn't sure I had the inner strength.

TWELVE

I banged on the glass door to Scott's laboratory, again. I wasn't going away until he let me in. We needed to sort this bloody mess out as soon as possible.

Scott's narrowed gaze finally surfaced behind the glass and the door swung open. "What are you doing here?"

I glared at him. "We need to talk."

Scott groaned and turned away, marching back across the sterile environment of stainless steel, white floors, and microscopes.

I let the door close and walked behind him. He sat back at his workstation and ignored me.

"Guess who I ran into today?" I asked while leaning back against the stainless-steel counter.

"Who?" Scott asked, not even bothering to look up from his microscope. He rotated knobs on the lens.

"Kane and Reid. They're on some sort of extended holiday. Catching up with the family, or something."

Kane and Reid were another perfect pair we hadn't seen in a long time.

Scott went unnaturally still, his hand frozen.

I continued, my heart still aching strangely from the conversation I'd had with the perfect pair from my father's side. "Did you know Kellie died last year?"

I hadn't known; no one had told me.

Kane and Reid were second or third cousins and rarely talked about on our side. Not that I would have listened, anyway. I'd always been insanely jealous of any perfect pair who had managed to find their mate.

Scott sighed and swivelled on his stool to face me. "Yeah, I did. I can't believe they're back in town, though. I thought..."

He looked away, his face pale in the stark light.

"You thought what?" I asked, crossing my arms over my chest.

He coughed and cleared his throat, finally looked back at me with a pained expression. "Didn't you listen when we were younger? This is one of the main reasons I never wanted to find our mate."

"What are you talking about?"

"Perfect pairs who are mated, are *linked*."

"Yeah. And?"

I thought that was the point of *the whole goddamn thing!*

I tapped my foot against the linoleum floor and bit my tongue against the need to yell. Getting words out of my twin was literally like pulling teeth sometimes.

"When the mate dies...the perfect pair die, too."

Shock skittled through my system. "What! How did I not know about that?"

Scott shrugged. "It's not really talked about because most families die later in life and are happy to perish together, anyway."

I swallowed; the life we'd led without our mate suddenly seemed like an all right alternative now.

I shook my head. Nope. I'd give anything to feel that connection with Ash again.

"Okay, so what's your point?" I said. "Don't give me any shit about not wanting to love Ash because of this. You've been living like a fucking corpse for twenty years now."

Scott swallowed hard, his Adam's apple bobbing up and down. "I know. Trust me, I know."

"Good." I grunted and nodded.

Scott continued. "My point is, it's been over a year for Kane and Reid. The longest any perfect pair has lasted was twelve months, absolute maximum."

"Ah well, they're only, what, thirty-something?"

Scott's gaze flickered a little. "Yeah, thirty-eight I think."

I let my arms drop. "Well, maybe they made a mistake about her being their mate? I don't know. Anyway, they're down here and they want to catch up, but we have bigger things to deal with at the moment. How are we going to get Ash back?"

Scott growled, the sound strangled and borderline menacing. I rumbled back, my lion baring its teeth.

"Just go away, Jack. The romance is over."

Not by a long shot.

I clenched my hands into two tight fists, anger billowing through my gut. "No fucking way it's over, you bloody fool! Get up off your ass and come with me to Brandon and Tyler's place."

After our fruitless night, I'd taken the day off, unlike my brother, and made some phone calls. I knew where she was, but I hadn't approached her yet. We needed a plan to get her back.

Scott stood up with stealth-like movements, and I took a step back and pivoted on my toes, readying for a fight. For the first time in my life, I wasn't sure what my brother was going to do.

"We had our night with her, and it's done, Jack. Why can't you just let it be?"

I relaxed my arms as my mouth dropped open.

Then the anger set in.

"Let it be? *Let it be!*" I slammed my fist into the metal table and jerked when I heard glass shatter nearby. I didn't give a shit what I'd just broken. "We have been missing a piece of us for forty fucking years. We finally found her, and you want to let her go? Didn't you feel *anything* Saturday night?"

He blinked a few times, and then looked away, his voice cracking when he spoke. "Of course, I did. But..."

I waited, my belly clenching with fear and anger. Oh, what I wouldn't give to plant my brother right into the wall. *"But what?"*

I bit my cheek until I tasted blood.

Scott straightened his shoulders and looked directly at me, all warmth gone from his eyes. "We aren't meant to be together, Jack. It's too hard. Too much water has gone under the bridge. Maybe you and Ash can work something out, but I can't."

I grabbed the closest thing to me, which was a heavy microscope, and threw it as hard as I could across the room with a roar. The microscope slammed into the wall with a loud crack.

"Fuck, Scott! No!" I roared again, hot anger spilling over every cell of my body. My skin was vibrating, and fur began to push through...

I couldn't shift here. It wasn't safe. If anyone from his work saw, his life would be over as he knew it.

Stop. Just... stop.

I forced the animal down, focusing my mind on Ash's smiling face, her tender kisses, her warm hands on my skin.

My humanity returned and I panted hard, twisting to glare at Scott. "This is on you, brother. You broke this. You and that stupid niece of mine. So, you fix it! Now. And know this. I will *never* forgive you if you don't at least *try*. She is our destiny, do you understand? *Ours*! And if you let her walk away over this stupid bullshit, I'll..."

I panted, running out of words as my anger peaked once again.

"You'll what, Jack?" Scott's words were soft in the room.

With a growl, I marched over to the exit and wrenched open the steel door. I turned around so I could throw my parting shot straight at him, angry snarls punctuating the words.

"I'll get in my car and drive to fucking Alaska and never look back. You *want* to wallow in your misery, don't you? Fuck that. You can wallow for the rest of your life, for all I care."

I slammed the door behind me and clenched my fists as I stormed out of the building and into the sunshine.

I closed my eyes, letting the heat and light filter through my skin and inside my soul.

I always tried to put my best face first. I got the most out of every situation because I wanted to. It was a conscious choice. People found it strange, but I found it easy to smile even in the worst situations.

But this was fucked up!

I started running, my arms moving as fast as they could. I desperately needed to shift into my animal form. My heart pumped as I weaved through the parking lot and made my way to the edge of the forest only a few blocks away.

I hated that I had to count on not just one person but two for my happiness.

It left me feeling powerless and totally out of control—which were two things I had sworn I'd never allow myself to be.

Scott

I lifted my trembling hand, mentally fighting the intense urge I had to run.

Instead, I knocked on the intricately carved wooden door.

Oh fuck, oh fuck.

My heart was thundering in my chest, and my brain was tearing me apart. There were so many different thoughts and emotions running through me that I felt like a ping pong ball in an Olympic match. My base instincts wanted me to turn and run, yet a stronger, more primal force made me stay planted firmly in place.

I had to do this for Jack, if for no other reason. That was enough.

The door swung open and Tyler greeted me with a smile. "Hey, Scott, how you doing?"

I waited, but he didn't invite me in. Instead, he crossed his arms over his chest and raised his eyebrows.

Great, so I've gotta go through you too? Like this isn't hard enough.

"Pretty good, Ty, how are you?"

Tyler laughed. The sound so vibrant, it almost brought tears to my eyes. I wanted to feel that way. To be able to make a sound that was so strong and carefree.

"Bloody awesome, actually," he said. "Married life definitely suits us."

He grinned, and I felt that stab to my heart. Was this really possible for Jack and me?

I cleared my throat and indicated inside Tyler and Brandon's house. "Is Ashleigh here?"

Tyler cocked his head, studying me before nodding. "Yeah, she is. You come to get the truck? I've got the keys."

He dangled Jack's keys in my face, and I reached up and took them. "Ah, no. But thanks for that.

Good, she was here. Jack had been right.

I waited for the invitation to come inside, but Tyler just stared at me.

My belly jumped and my heart beat a little faster. It'd been so long since I fought for something, anything, that actually mattered.

And no matter what I tried to tell myself and the rest of the world, Ashleigh mattered.

I let out a pent-up breath. "I need to see her, Ty. Can I come in?"

Tyler stepped back and waved toward the kitchen. "Of course. Come on in."

I stepped over the threshold, giving him a playful shove. "What's with the bodyguard treatment?"

He punched me in the shoulder and chuckled. "I'm the easy one. You have to get past my wife next."

I stopped and looked into the house with a nervous smile. "Are you serious?"

Tyler pushed at me. "Yep, and you think we're the lions? Ha! You haven't seen a *mate* protecting *her* family yet."

"Oh, shit." My heart fell as I trudged along the hallway.

My mother had always been pretty fierce when it came to her husband and children; would Laura be the same? The answer to that was in the slightly evil sounding chuckle behind me.

I stepped into the kitchen. Ash sat with Laura, drinking from a mug. My spine straightened as I stared at her. A wave of something quite primitive, similar to possession, passed over me.

Would Ash be like Laura and my mother? Would she attack to protect those she loved? Like a true woman and alpha female should. That would mean she was the complete opposite of my ex-wife, who chose to tear me down any time she was able.

Both women turned toward me, and I froze, pinned by the pain in the depths of Ash's blue eyes.

"Hi," I said.

A smile trembled on her lips. "Hey there, Mr. I-turn-into-a-lion."

My mouth turned up into a grin at the teasing tone behind her words. Whatever I'd prepared myself for, this wasn't it.

"I came over to check on you and explain," I said. "I'm so sorry we didn't tell you about our shifting abilities earlier. And I can't even begin to explain how sorry I am about how you were forced to find out like that."

Her face fell and she glared at me, that strength and fire I loved about her returning. "You mean when your..." She hesitated, and I could almost hear the words *nasty* and *childish* in the air. Then she cleared her throat. "When your *daughter* came in ranting and raving and got so mad, she made all three of you shift?"

My cheeks heated. Meaghan was a manipulative miniature version of her mother, and it cut deep to know she'd hurt Ash with her childish behavior.

I exhaled sharply. "Ah, yes. We should have explained it before any of that."

Laura stood up and glared at me. "You both handled the whole thing badly, Scott. I expected better from you and Jack."

I raised my eyebrows. She barely knew us. Who was she to judge me? I ignored her comment and continued to address Ashleigh.

"I'm very sorry about Meaghan, but children—teenage daughters, especially—are very temperamental."

Both Laura and Ash grumbled, and I took a deep breath in through my nose. That wasn't the important point here.

"Ash, can we go somewhere private and talk?" I said. "Or can I take you out for dinner?"

Laura's hand slid over to Ash's and she glared at me. "No, she's staying here. I know you've had your fair share of shit, Scott, but Ash isn't strong enough to deal with it at the moment."

Ash shook her head. "Stop, Laura, it's okay…"

"No!" Laura shot Ash a stern look before returning her hard gaze to me. "Ash just escaped a poisonous environment with her ex-husband, and I won't let you subject her to an even worse one. If you can't be honest, or control that family of yours, then perfect pair or not, you need to back off until you can."

Oh fuck. This is even worse than I thought.

I hadn't asked much about Ash's past and guilt hit me like a punch to the gut. I'd been so focused on my own scars, I hadn't even considered that she'd have some of her own.

I was also used to ignoring Meaghan's teenage tantrums, and I hadn't considered the effect her outburst would have on Ashleigh—especially if she'd come from a poisonous environment.

I'd hoped it would be as simple as apologizing about the shifter thing, and then taking her home to Jack.

Ash finally lifted her eyes to mine and for the first time, I saw the fragility of my mate.

I wanted to make it right. I wanted to take away that pain in her expression. "I'm ready to be completely honest with you, Ash. Please give me a chance to explain everything."

I held out my hand and waited, my arm trembling as adrenaline pumped through my system.

Ash stood and moved over to me. Relief flowed over me like a warm shower.

"Ashleigh, you know you don't have to talk to him alone," Laura said. "You can take Brandon if you want. He's in the garage."

Brandon? Seriously? He was an even bigger meathead than Jack! As if Ash needed his protection. I wasn't going to hurt my mate.

I growled a little at Laura, and Ash squeezed my hand. "It's all cool, Laura. You told me they wouldn't hurt me even in lion form, yeah?"

Laura nodded with a begrudging look. "Well, you can use the backyard if you want. There's a table and chairs out there."

I inhaled through my nose and nodded sharply. I wasn't sure I should speak at the moment. My tone would give away my feelings toward Laura a little too obviously.

"Come on, Scott." Ash tugged my hand outside, into the warm air.

I took a deep breath and let my shoulders slump. "I can't believe she was going to send Brandon out to chaperon us, for fuck's sake!"

Ash chuckled and dropped into one of the padded outdoor chairs. "What's wrong? Couldn't take him in a fight?"

I growled, my lion ready for anything. "At the moment, I think I could."

She laughed and patted the seat next to her. "But he's the brawn of his pair and you're the brains of yours. I'd expect you to work out a way to get out of it without using your fists."

I bent over and grabbed her face, kissing her hard and fast.

"We have lots of similarities too," I said, standing upright.

I fell into the chair next to her, my hormones raging, my breathing fast and erratic. One moment I'd convinced myself I was getting Ash back for Jack, and then the next, I couldn't help grabbing her and acting possessive and needy.

"You okay?" Ash's gentle voice and soft hand on my arm cleared my mind, and I focused on her.

I reached up and cupped Ashleigh's face in my hands. "I really am sorry about Meaghan, Ash. Her mother uses her like a puppet to do her dirty work. It's a horrible situation."

Ash nodded. "Yes, I can imagine it is, and it's a situation I'm not sure I want to be forced into the middle of."

I cocked my head to the side, my belly jumping. "What do you mean?"

She withdrew her hand from mine, and I almost cried out as a wall came down between us. What the fuck was happening here?

"I think I can handle the shifting thing. Laura's explained it, and it doesn't seem like such a big deal now that I've had time to get over the initial shock of it."

So, what's the problem, then?

She bit her lip and looked away, her generous mouth pulling down on one side. "But this blended family thing is going to be so hard to live with."

She sounded so defeated. My heart, which had begun to settle down, surged up into a higher gear. She couldn't break our connection due to my children, surely? She hadn't even met them all yet!

"We don't have to blend anything, really," I said. "Jack and I will look after our kids when we have to, and we'll focus on you the rest of the time."

Now that I thought about it, that would be the perfect solution.

With me and Jack being a pair, one of us would always be with Ash. She could still have everything she needed.

Maybe it really was possible to make it work, and I wouldn't necessarily have to live with her and Jack. I could visit, or maybe build something nearby. We could work out a balance for everyone to be happy.

Ash stared at me and then shook her head. "You don't understand me at all, do you?"

I cleared my throat and shifted in my chair. I needed to be very careful here; I could practically feel the land mines set to blow around me.

"We only met on Friday," I said. "I'm not going to lie and claim to know everything about you—that's impossible in the short time we've had together. But what I do know about you, I like. A lot. I also know you are the one for me and Jack. That is enough to build on, to create an incredible relationship in the future between the three of us, but we need time to do that."

Wow. I blinked. When had I decided she was the one for me?

The first time you touched her, you idiot!

I grimaced and focused back on my woman. It was true, I had a long way to go to understand her, but the fact that she was designed for Jack and me was obvious.

"I know that, but you don't understand," she said. "I want to love you, all of you, with all my heart. That means being a part of your lives. All of it. I don't want to ignore the fact that you have three children. I want to be part of their lives too! And with an ex-wife like yours, how the hell are we going to make it work?"

I laughed. I didn't mean to, but the sound just burst out of me.

She glared and crossed her arms over her beautiful breasts.

"Come here." I grabbed her elbow and pulled hard, arranging her so she was across my lap, all stiff and indignant.

"Don't make fun of me!" Ash groaned.

I wrapped my arms around her wriggling body and chuckled. "My gorgeous woman, I adore you. Please stop, I'm only laughing because you have more heart than any woman I've ever met."

She slapped my shoulder before settling to glare at me. "What the hell are you talking about now?"

I moved my hands up to her face and cupped her cheeks, loving the feel of her warm skin. "You want to love me that much? Bloody hell, woman, where have you been all my life?"

The soppy words kept spilling out and I knew I should feel like a fool, but I was too happy. She really was the intelligent, loving, sensual woman I'd always hoped for. She was our mate, our perfect woman. Now I had to win back her trust.

She slipped her hands around my neck and cocked her head. "Aren't you the least bit concerned about how we're going to get this to work?"

I pressed my lips to hers and moaned as she responded with a sweet little groan of her own.

I pulled back and stared at her. "No, I'm not. Jack and I tried to make our own lives separately and failed miserably, and I finally know why."

She grinned at me, a playful light entering her sparkling blue eyes. "And why's that?"

I growled, letting my lion come out to strut a little. "Because we were both meant to love *you*!"

She giggled and wrapped herself tighter around me, kissing me until we were both panting.

"Shall we go home?" I asked her, rubbing my nose against hers and hoping to hell I'd done enough to convince her to give us another chance.

She slid off my lap and stood up on wobbly legs. "Yes, but don't think you're totally off the hook yet. I want to see you guys in lion form, and you have to prove that I'm safe around you."

"And I'd like to learn more about your past, Ash. I'm sorry I haven't asked more about you up to this point."

From what Laura had said earlier, it sounded like I had a lot to learn about her past. But we'd get there.

She nodded, so I took her hand and proceeded to lead her inside to get her things. "It will be our pleasure to show you our lions, sweetheart. We could *never* hurt you, in human or shifter form."

If she wanted us to shift for her. Then done.

She wanted us to beg her forgiveness. Then done.

The only thing we wouldn't do, was let her go.

THIRTEEN

I paced up and down Scott's kitchen, sweat on my brow and adrenaline pumping through my blood stream. I'd gone to the gym, but it hadn't helped to quell the building panic. I was slowly losing control, and my bloody brother was nowhere to be found.

My phone rang and I picked it up within the first vibration. *Scott*.

"Where the fuck are you?"

Scott's chuckle made its way down the phone and I slid onto one of the kitchen stools as a wave of relief passed over me. Something good had happened.

"I'm in my car on my way home," he said. "Where are you, brother?"

I cleared my throat. I hadn't heard a happy tone in Scott's voice for a long time. "Ah, I'm at your place. I let myself in."

"Good, we'll be there soon, then we can sort all this stuff out tonight."

Thump, thump, thump. My heart hammered and the vibrations pulsed in my ears.

"We?"

Could it be possible? Had my brother done the right thing and fixed things up with our mate?

"Yeah, I'm bringing Ash home with me," he said, and I could hear his grin.

Oh, thank you!

"Awesome, see you guys soon."

I hung up the phone and put both hands on my knees. "Thank you, thank you," I whispered.

I wiped away the moisture that leaked out of my eyes and laughed at myself.

It was finally time to start living our lives, as long as we could convince Ash we would be good together as a threesome.

Ash

SCOTT RUSHED AROUND and opened the car door for me, took my hand in his, and led me up the path to his house. I was still trembling, but it was with anticipation rather than fear. It made me feel alive and reminded me that I really was awake. I'd spent hours thinking about a return to my old life. My house, my business, my friends. And the thought had filled me with dread.

Now that I was back in Scott's arms, everything felt right once again.

As if I could just walk away from everything I'd ever wanted, plus more. Two men who would love me for who I was, and who made me feel cherished and important in their lives.

Now, thanks to this impromptu wedding trip, I was closer than I'd ever been before to that dream. Because if I was honest, I'd had more moments of pure love with Jack and Scott in these few days than I'd had in ten years with my ex-husband.

Surely, there was the possibility of so much more in the years to come, if that was what we'd accomplished in mere days.

The front door swung open as we approached and Jack bounced out wearing jeans and a gray sleeveless shirt, looking sexier than any man had a right to.

"You're back." He grabbed me and swung me up into his arms.

I squealed like a schoolgirl as my feet left the ground, and he planted kisses on my face at a frantic pace.

"Oh, sweetheart, you're here," he said. "You're really here."

He thrust his tongue into my mouth and grabbed my ass, his movements seeming unsophisticated and desperate.

I pushed at his chest, feeling squashed and overwhelmed. "Please, Jack. Can we go inside?"

"Oh, yeah. Sure." He adjusted his grip on me, placing a hand around my waist, lifting me and swinging me up properly into his arms.

I shrieked, and then shook my head as he opened the door and carried me over the threshold and down the hallway.

My big footballer was in such a rush!

I wanted one specific thing from them both before we got intimate again, which I knew was probably going to happen soon.

Jack's obvious need was creating an incredibly delicious masculine scent and I knew that the best way for us all to feel more secure about this relationship was to get as close as possible. But whether that was best done through sex right now, I wasn't one hundred percent sure.

The men's physicality had been so overwhelming so far, it might be smarter to take it back a notch.

Once Jack finally put me down, I moved into the modern lounge room and across the room to gain some distance.

Jack walked forward, his hands outstretched, palm up. "What's wrong? I don't know what Scott told you, so I'm not sure what you need."

My poor sweetheart sounded pained, and he probably was. He'd done nothing to hurt me except omit to tell me about their shifting ability.

Which I kind of understood, considering the shock value of that information.

He'd given me so much already, and he didn't deserve any more grief.

"It's all good, Jack. Scott explained everything."

I made a mental note to ask Jack about his kids and ex-wife at a later date. His initial explanations seemed to indicate that they wouldn't be the same kind of problem that Scott's might be, but I really should check that out and not just make assumptions.

"Well, why'd you pull away, then?" His shoulder and arm muscles flexed and bulged as he shifted from foot to foot. He looked as uncomfortable as a cat on a hot tin roof.

I burst into giggles at the thought.

That's a little too close to reality.

He cocked his head to the side, a grin stretching across his face. "What's funny, beautiful?"

I shook my head. "Doesn't matter. I want to see you guys in lion form again, but this time I want you to let me touch you, if that's okay?"

"Oh, that's easy." Jack growled, the sound deep and sexy, and a shiver coursed up my spine. Then he began ripping at his clothes.

Scott entered the room and stopped, staring at Jack. "Um, what's happening?"

I smiled at him, putting both hands on my hips and striking a pose. "I want to see you guys in lion form, and you have to do what I say since you scared the shit out of me yesterday."

Scott chuckled. "Anything you want, my love."

His eyes burned with lust as he undressed.

I shifted my gaze to where Jack should have been, only to find him gone. "Jack?"

Very timidly, a mountain lion stepped around the couch and lowered his body until he rested his head on his front paws in front of me.

He was huge, and intimidating. And utterly gorgeous.

"Oh, wow." I was frozen in place, adrenaline pumping through my system as a second cinnamon-colored cat stalked up beside the first and lay down in the same position.

God, they're beautiful.

I swallowed the lump stuck in my throat, the hairs on my arms prickling in instinctive fear. These animals could tear me apart in a heartbeat if they chose to.

"Jack?" I asked, voice quivering.

The lion on the right raised its head before returning to rest it on his paws.

"Scott?"

The lion on the left stood up and purred before lying back down.

"Wow," I said, breathless. "You guys...are *stunning*. Can I touch you?"

Both cats rolled over and exposed their bellies like the tamest of house pets.

I giggled, unable to believe they could really understand me so easily in this form. I crept forward, my knees shaking.

The powerful lions in front of me lay perfectly still as I reached out with trembling hands and ran my fingers through the soft fur over their ribcages.

I began to laugh. What an incredible moment in time. Not only could I touch these men, I could enjoy their lions whenever I wanted to.

It was still completely surreal, and I needed more time to adjust. "Okay, please change back. I want my men."

Their cinnamon-and-white fur melted away as my perfect pair reappeared as naked and gorgeous men, crouched before me.

Both of them stood, and then Jack reached forward and stroked his hands along my thighs, his touch electric and hot over my leg. "Will you mate with us, Ashleigh? Give yourself to us and commit to being ours?"

Really? Already?

I looked between my men, my heart aching with the pleasure

and compliment such a question gave me. But it was too soon. "You know I adore you," I said. "Both of you. But I need more time to decide. Is that all right?"

The men looked at each other.

Jack seemed disappointed but there was something in Scott's expression that made me feel as though I'd made the right choice.

Scott took a small step forward. "Is this about the kids, Ash? I know Meaghan would have upset you with all that talk about her mom."

I glanced away, not really wanting to open that wound at the moment. "I know how teenagers can be, and I know she would have a warped view of how your marriage was."

Scott nodded. "She does. My marriage was torture. I only stayed as long as I did for my kids."

I swallowed hard and glanced at Jack, who laughed and put up his hands. "Don't look at me. I got out early, and my ex and I are pretty amicable. I'll talk to my sons before they come anywhere near you, but they're pretty chilled-out boys."

I smiled at my hunky man, imagining how beautiful his sons would be.

He took a step forward. "So, does that sort everything out?"

I blinked at him. "Ah…"

No. Not really.

Jack opened his mouth, but Scott beat him to the punch. "Take your time. We'll wait as long as you need us to. Forever, if we have to. We're not going to give up on you, Ash."

Jack nodded and huffed a little. My poor impatient lion.

"Bed?" Jack reached for me with his powerful hands.

I nodded slowly, my heart soaring with love for these men. "Yes, but no sex tonight."

He jerked back, but nodded slowly after a moment.

Scott grabbed my hand. "Whatever you need, Ash."

I shook my head, wanting to explain. "I want to, believe me. But

I've had a huge couple of days, and I need to just be held and feel close to you both. Can we do that?"

"Yes." Jack's voice was hoarse. "It'll be tough, but we can do that."

"We can," Scott agreed, and my love for them bloomed even brighter in that moment.

It was still light out, but we all went to bed. They undressed me down to my knickers and cradled me with their strong naked bodies, one on each side of me. They allowed me full access to touch and feel them as I desired.

I spoke softly to them as I enjoyed their powerful muscles and soft skin, but never once did I feel pressured or inadequate because of my no-sex rule.

They returned all of my love, giving me intimacy and reassurance —exactly what I needed. Every cell in my body was buzzing with happiness and light.

They massaged me and touched me for hours, until I fell into a deep, restful sleep. My dreams of what life *could* become were slowly coming true.

Scott

THE HEAT of my morning coffee seeped through the ceramic mug and warmed my hands. A sigh escaped my lips, and a lightness of heart I hadn't felt in over twenty years invaded my chest.

Ash had changed everything.

Only a week ago, every morning, I had to pull myself painfully out of bed, dreading the day to come.

My work was great, my home was clean, and I had the freedom to do whatever I wanted. Everyday. But a terrible feeling of emptiness had occupied my body and mind every second of every day.

This morning, the emptiness was gone.

I inhaled through my nose and breathed out through my mouth. My usually busy brain was completely at peace. A full night of affection, kisses, and loving words had been enough to convince me that Ashleigh really was our intended mate.

The woman had been custom-made for us. As we had been, for her. We'd never been this happy, and the best part was that it was only the beginning. We had our whole life ahead of us, and I could honestly say that my woman was the most incredible female I'd ever met in my life.

Fate, it seemed, had been kind to us after all.

My phone began to ring, and I glanced down.

Kerry. My heart sank. *Great.*

Negative thoughts poured into my mind, and my belly clenched. What did she want? Should I even answer? It was seven o'clock in the morning. Maybe something was wrong with the kids? Damn it! I had to pick up, just in case.

With a grimace, I pressed the green button, sluggishly pulling up the mental barriers I always needed when talking with my ex-wife. "Hello?"

"What the fuck is this I hear about you and Jack finding your mate? You always said *I* was your mate!"

My skull squeezed around my brain, and my eyes ached. I *had* said that, to try and reassure her that she didn't need to be so insecure all the time.

It hadn't worked. Her jealousy and pettiness had ripped us apart, destroying our relationship from the inside out.

"We didn't work out for more than one reason, Kerry, and the main one is probably because Jack and I are a perfect pair," I said, keeping my voice even. "The legend always said we'd find one woman to suit us both."

And of course, you're a fucking bitch, but you won't accept that as a reason.

"What a load of shit! You never believed in those fairy tales before."

I took a deep breath and let it out slowly. My blood pressure was rising just listening to that high-pitched voice of hers. "That's true, I didn't. But I've been proven wrong."

"You?" She scoffed loudly. "The perfect, intelligent, oh-so-talented Scott Tanner? You're never wrong, remember?"

I clenched my hand into a fist. "I'm wrong, and often, but unlike some, I'm willing to admit to it when I am."

"Unlike me, you mean? That's right, keep telling me how it's all my fault, when we both know it's not. You gave up, remember? You walked away from me and the kids that you said you loved! You promised me you'd never leave me."

I gripped the phone and squeezed my eyes shut, remembering the night I'd promised her that. All those years ago when I was sure I could make her love me.

Enough at least so that she'd be a good wife and a decent mother to our brood. I'd known on some level I'd been wrong, and later, when the choice had come to either kill myself to get away from the depression and pain, or move out, I'd made the latter choice.

Moving out and starting again had been harder than simply ending my life. And if I was honest, I'd regretted that choice, many times. During the past five years, I'd lived alone and Kerry had continued to torture me, compounding the loneliness and depression.

Not anymore.

Thanks to Ash, I felt no guilt about my ex-wife.

I also felt no need to placate her. With a smile, I cut off my ex-wife's rambling. "It's been five years. You really need to move on. Now, do you need something, Kerry? I'm busy."

She growled through the phone, and my lion rose inside me.

God, how we'd fought in the past. Always words, but there'd been nights when my lion had risen and roared through me, demanding I rip her limb from limb.

It had been willpower and some luck that I'd never given in to the urge.

"How dare you threaten our daughter?" she continued. "And over that fat whore you and your brother are fucking? You know that's sick, right? You are totally perverted. We will never forgive you, and I will make sure..."

Her voice disappeared as I did something I'd never done before: I hung up on her.

There was a small amount of pride at the move, but mostly... there was pain. I may have lost the family I'd sacrificed everything for. Losing the stress of Kerry was a relief, but my children were my life.

I flicked my phone to silent and threw it in the direction of the lounge room, the phone making a thud as it hit the carpet.

I wrapped my hands back around my coffee mug and searched for the peace I'd woken with this morning.

Acid burned in my gut, and I groaned. She'd got in, the fucking bitch. My ex-wife was like a leech. Feeding on my pain. Draining every drop of energy out of my blood.

I sipped my coffee, feeling the tension in my shoulders gather and tighten. "Shit."

I finished my coffee, trying to think of anything but Kerry. When the happiness I'd woken with didn't return, I moved to my study and got stuck into my work.

My lion was still vibrating with rage. Would I ever be free to be happy?

FOURTEEN

ASH

I stretched and groaned, deliciously warm and being snuggled by a big, cuddly male.

"Good morning." I smiled as Jack kissed my neck and bumped his pelvis against me, his hard cock pressing into my bum.

My body responded instantly, my pussy tightening and pulsing in anticipation of what was to come.

"Good morning to you too," he said.

I smiled up at my beautiful footballer and reached out for my scientist.

The other side of the bed was cold, and I couldn't stop my hands from searching the space. I didn't like the fact he was gone already.

Scott had said he was committed to being with me, but there was something still holding him back. It was time to work on that.

I pulled myself out of bed,

Jack groaned behind me. "Where are you going, beautiful?"

I wasn't quite sure. "I think I need to find Scott."

He should have still been in bed with us, especially after the awesome night we'd had. Where was he?

Jack collapsed back on our bed.

I pulled on the gray singlet Jack had left on the floor, the cotton floating down over my body and covering me to mid-thigh.

I blew him a kiss as I headed out the bedroom door.

"Well, get back here quickly," he called out after me.

I giggled as I moved through the house, looking for my tortured hero.

Last night had been amazing, intimate, and beautiful. But there were still things I needed to learn about Scott. His situation—and his emotions—weren't as simple as Jack.

With my big footballer, most of his scars were on the surface and he was honest and comfortable with them. I knew what I was getting with him.

Scott was different.

I turned the corner into Scott's office and found him in front of a computer screen. "Here you are, my lovely one."

The words flowed from my mouth without conscious direction. He whirled around, his face pale.

I needed to bridge the gap, and quickly.

"Good morning." I gave him my brightest smile and cupped his cheeks, kissing him with all the love in my heart.

He moaned and kissed me back, slipping his tongue into my mouth so I sucked on it, revelling in his sweet flavor and the way he shivered beneath my hands.

I loved how he did that.

It was almost as though he'd never been touched before.

I pulled back slowly, rubbing my nose against his. "Couldn't wait to get working?"

He shrugged, his mouth pulling down on the side. "I can't sleep past six, so I got up to have a shower and a coffee, but I planned to come back after that."

I glanced at the clock. It was past eight. "What happened, then?"

His mouth pulled tight again and I sighed. He was hiding things from me.

"Let's go sit on the couch," I said.

I didn't let him answer. I simply turned and walked back to the lounge room, heading over to the couch. I dropped down onto the soft leather, and waited for him.

It took a moment, but he finally entered the room and took a seat opposite me, his hands clenched in his lap.

"Where's Jack?" he asked, his right leg jiggling in an annoying way.

"He's probably gone back to sleep." I shrugged to indicate that Jack was the least of my concerns. "You all right?"

He mimicked my shrug and glanced away then back with a bleak look in his eyes. "Yeah, of course."

I needed to push forward, but I didn't know enough yet to even guess right. Or did I?

There only seemed to be one thing that made Scott flinch—a certain woman who'd birthed his offspring. "Did your ex or one of your kids call you?"

His head came up, his eyes widening.

Yes! Right on target.

"Ah, yeah," he said. "How'd you know? My ex called this morning."

I made a disgusted noise. That woman sounded like hell in a skirt. "And what did the bitch want?"

A shocked laugh came out of him, while I huffed and crossed my arms.

"You know she's nothing to you anymore, Scott. If you've got me, you can let go of whatever link you have to her."

His face grew taut. "I don't have any connections to her anymore, except for the kids, of course."

I grimaced. This was a hard conversation for us to have, but it had to be done.

"I don't have any kids, so I can't really imagine what it must feel like to be linked to someone like that, but I know that people only have power over you when you allow them to have it."

Scott grimaced. "I don't let her, it's just...I don't know."

I flexed my fingers and took another slow breath. "Okay, let's leave that topic alone. Can we talk about you and me? You feel colder this morning. Further away."

He stared at me and didn't speak, so I plowed forward, calling on every instinct I had to guide me. "Are you worried about our connection not lasting, or me preferring your twin? Or what? I just can't shake the feeling that you're not committed the way Jack is."

I could practically *feel* Jack's love like a never-ending fountain of heat and power. Scott was only giving me what he had to; what he thought was enough.

It wasn't.

I needed his *all.* That sort of imbalance would never work in our family.

"I don't know what you mean," he said, sounding defensive.

I laughed. I had to. Crying was the only other option and I didn't want to do that. "Oh, please. I know you're holding back on me—on us—which is the main reason I can't fully mate with you guys yet. How can I when you don't really want me?"

My voice broke as tears gathered in my throat. I swallowed them down.

Scott barely moved as he said, "Of course, I want you, Ashleigh. You're our mate."

A pressure gasket burst in my chest and I screamed at him. "I'm not going to stay just because I'm your mate! This relationship has to be about love and affection, not obligation and duty!"

I pushed back and crossed my arms over my chest, my breathing labored. I forced myself to continue, though my instincts were yelling at me to get up and walk out on him. He was just sitting there doing *nothing*!

"I am fully committed to staying here and making our life work, despite the horrible ex-wives, possibly bitchy stepchildren, and a shifter world I am petrified of," I said. "What the hell do you have to be afraid of?"

Scott opened his mouth, and then closed it again.

I cried out in exasperation. What else did I have to say to make this extremely intelligent man understand? "For fuck's sake, Scott! What is it? What is the worst thing that could happen?"

My words echoed around the room and I glared at him.

He moved from side to side and swallowed several times, his Adam's apple bobbing like a buoy in the ocean. "You'll turn out like all the rest of them, Ash. I know you will."

"I will what? Scott, tell me!"

My eyes burned with tears, and my heart ached for the man before me.

"You'll flip," he said. "You'll turn into a bitch."

Wow. That was not what I was expecting.

"Why would you assume that? Did all your other lovers make you feel the way I do?"

He stared at me with intense green eyes and shook his head slowly.

"You felt the perfect pair mate electricity thing with other women?"

Again, that shake of his head, more vigorously this time.

I was playing a dangerous game here. Scott was sitting on the precipice of a cliff. He was either going to dive off and into our love, or he'd back away and never approach the cliff edge again.

I continued onward. "Have you ever met a woman like me? Who wanted to hold you, love you, discuss concepts and ideas with you?"

He shook his head again, and I laughed a little, my heart in my throat.

We'd shared so much, even in such a short space of time. I knew, deep down to the depths of my soul, that I was designed for these men. What was he really afraid of?

"Scott, you are the most logical man I've ever met. You're gorgeous and intelligent, and I know your heart is capable of loving me with everything you have."

He nodded, and then looked away when his eyes began shimmering with tears.

Was that the way through to him? To tell him how happy I was?

"Scott, I am so happy, and it is all because of you and Jack."

He grimaced, and I knew I'd hit another scar. I moved around the coffee table and sat closer to him.

I slid my hand into his, the glow of our connection warming my skin. "Scott, I can't say I love you more than your twin. We're not designed that way. But I love you just as much. You're perfect complements and, between you both, you meet every one of my needs. When I have a problem with my business, I know I can turn to you. Jack can joke me out of any bad mood, and you can touch me until I cry at the sheer joy of it. Why would I ever jeopardize any of that by being a bitch?"

He let out a laugh that was almost cruel. "Because degrading me is the best way to control me."

Tears welled and slid down my cheeks. What sort of life had this man led?

"I don't want to control you. That's not how I want to keep you by my side, Scott. I intend to make you so happy that you'll never want to leave me. It will be your *choice*."

He looked away, clearing his throat with rough, broken sounds. "Yeah, well, that would be a first."

I swallowed awkwardly around the lump in my throat. This was the harder bit, cracking open my heart and hoping to God he didn't want to add to my pain.

"I spent years with a man who kept trying to squash me down and change me into something he wanted me to be." My voice faltered at the end.

Without hesitation, Scott pulled me closer, drawing me against his warm body and over into his lap.

I wiped away the tears with the backs of my hands and took some calming breaths so that I could keep talking.

I looked up into his shimmering gaze and cupped the side of his head, stroking my thumb through the silver hair at his temple. "I love you so much, Scott, and I know you're what I need. Love for me is putting the other person's needs above my own. I'll never hurt you, not on purpose. I feel gutted when you're in pain."

Something shifted through his expression and he buried his face into my hair. I wrapped my arms around his strong frame, holding him to me.

He spoke against my neck, his breath hot on my skin.

"If you change, Ashleigh, it'll kill me." He pulled back and stared up at me with eyes as deep as a lake. "I already love you more than I've ever loved anyone. If you turn on me now..."

I gripped his head and stared at him, speaking the words that were screamed from my heart. "I will never turn on you."

We kissed like we'd never get the chance again, tongues sparring in each other's mouths, hands grappling, and groans breaking the air around us.

"Bed. Now. I need to show you how much you mean to me." He growled at me as he stood up, then swung me up into his arms and walked toward the bedroom.

My heart was swimming in happiness and light, begging with me to end this separation and fully commit to my new family.

Scott

IT WILL BE YOUR CHOICE, she said. *Your choice.*

I'd never felt like I had a choice, before now.

My heart pounded in my chest like the thumping of a bass guitar, the vibrations ricocheting through my body from the center all the way to my fingertips.

"You really want me, sweetheart? All of me?" The words rolled out of me without restraint and I kissed her possessively, tasting her distinctive sweetness as I strode down the hallway.

. . .

SHE NODDED and gripped my neck tight, panting and flushed in my arms. "Yes. Please, Scott."

Fuck, she was beautiful!

I kneed open the door, and Jack sat bolt upright in bed.

"Is she okay?" he asked. "What happened?"

I chuckled, the feeling of joy strange in my belly. I tossed Ash into the center of the bed, letting a rumbling laugh emerge when she bounced into Jack.

"Have I missed something?" Jack wrapped his arms around her, sliding his hands up under her long singlet and exposing her soft belly and the gorgeous thighs I loved to be between.

I pulled off my shirt and pushed my pants down, my body itching to be completely naked. "No, just our mate pushing me into manning up."

Ash glared at me. "Hey!"

I laughed again, the stretching of my lips and cheeks feeling awkward and strange. "It's true, though. You were right."

I smiled down at the people who were now my family and moaned as my hand found my stiffening cock. I stroked the aching flesh slowly.

"My past has been holding me back, but you both deserve more than that. You're going to be my family now, aren't you?" I looked straight at Ash.

She nodded, and then said, "Yes, and I know we haven't talked about kids yet, but do you guys want more?"

I glanced at my twin, whose eyes widened with surprise.

I shrugged. "If you'd asked me last week, I would have said no way. But with you, Ash, I'm excited about creating a family."

And if that meant more babies, more nappies, more screaming teenagers, then I was in.

Ash giggled as Jack stripped the singlet off her completely, grabbing her abundant boobs with easy familiarity.

"So, by family, you just mean, more children?" she asked, looking between us.

I shared a look with my brother. No, we didn't just mean that. "No, we mean a true family. One where our woman loves us and our children. A house full of laughter and happiness."

"Ow." I grabbed my chest as something wonderful exploded inside my heart, spreading out like rippling waves in a pond. What was happening? My knees shook and I staggered, reaching out and grabbing the doorframe to steady myself.

"You okay?" Ash asked, her voice urgent. *Was I okay?* I rubbed my chest, the strange feeling receding. In its place was the lightness I'd felt this morning, filling me up until I was completely encompassed with it. My head was now clear of all negativity.

"Wow, yeah, I'm very much okay. A family with you is exactly what I want," I said.

The bliss spread through my whole body, relaxing all of my muscles.

Jack grunted as he continued to caress our woman. "Me, too."

Ash wiped away tears on her cheeks, and I crawled onto the bed, pulling her into my arms and kissing her. "Are you ready to mate with us now? Bond with us so that, from this moment on, we'll never be able to survive without you?"

Ash nodded slowly, two more tears slipping down her flushed cheeks.

"Yes, please. But tell me more what will happen."

Oh, thank God for that.

"Jack and I will both be inside you at the same time, and then at the climax, we will bite your shoulders and seal our pact."

She smiled. "Does it hurt?"

I shook my head. "From what I've been told, no. But we've never mated before with anyone. Maybe we should have asked Laura?"

Ash smiled again. "I bet it doesn't hurt."

"Then let's find out, shall we?"

I pushed my lover down and kissed a trail down her chest until I found the slope of her breast. I loved how voluptuous she was, and I couldn't wait to see our babe suckling her in the same way.

I looked over my mate. "Damn, you're beautiful. I love your flesh."

She turned with a moan, and I took her nipple into my mouth, drawing on the bud.

"Oh, my…" She arched her back and I sucked harder, loving the way her hands tugged on my hair and held me to her.

Jack's shoulder pressed into me as he moved up to kiss her, so I headed south, giving over her upper body to my brother.

I inserted my tongue into her belly button and smiled as I looked up and watched Jack plump up her breasts and tweak the tips with his fingers and mouth.

I moved even lower, running my tongue down the center of her and circling her clit.

"Ah! Scott!" She gasped and bucked beneath me as I explored her flesh, loving the sweet taste and strong scent of my gorgeous woman.

I licked down between her open petals and tasted her wetness. She groaned, and then gasped.

Jack rested on his knees beside her head and slid his cock between her lips.

I continued to love her body, reveling in her tight grip on my hair and her wiggles of pleasure.

"Scott," Ash panted, her voice slightly muffled as she pulled away from Jack, "come up here too."

I crawled up beside her, tweaking her nipples on the way.

I knelt next to her head opposite my brother and groaned when she grabbed my erect cock in her hand and began pumping me while she sucked him.

I let my eyes close and moved my hips in time with her tugging.

Wet heat engulfed my cock, and my eyes flew open to watch Ash's mouth working my flesh.

"God, Ash…that is fucking…exquisite."

My gorgeous, giving woman was driving me insane. Tingles of

pleasure raced up my spine and my cock throbbed with every suck and tug of her mouth and tongue.

She alternated twice more and by then my cock was bright red and making pearly drops at the slit.

It was time to bind Ash to us forever.

FIFTEEN

I licked the drop of salty cream from the tip of Scott's gorgeous cock and swallowed with relish.

Damn that was yum. Must be a shifter thing.

I grabbed tighter to his hot flesh as he pulled away from me.

I looked up at him, worry threading through my heart. "Everything okay?"

Scott smiled down at me. "Let's make love to you, sweetheart."

Absolutely!

"Oh, yes."

I let go of my lovers and watched them both move off the mattress to stand at the end of the bed. Scott grabbed two condoms out of a nearby drawer and handed one to Jack. Panic surfaced, bubbling up in my blood like air in water. I didn't want that protection or barrier between us. Not anymore.

"No," I said, lifting my head. "Please, I want to feel you both inside me properly."

The men glanced at each other in silent communication.

I shuddered with desire when they both turned to stare at me with looks that showed more heat and lust than I'd ever seen on anyone.

Jack growled at me. "I'd love that, beautiful girl, but you could get pregnant right away."

I nodded, too aroused to laugh at the way he said it. I knew how babies were made. He didn't need to tell me.

"It's not the right time for me so the probability is low, but I don't care. I want your children whenever you want to give them to me."

Scott grabbed the condoms back off his brother and threw them over his shoulder. "We want that too. Your genetics are too amazing not to breed with. Your babies will be kind, beautiful, and brilliant."

I flushed, the true meaning of his scientific words warming my heart.

He crawled onto the bed, lay on his back, and gestured to me to get on top of him. "Come ride me, sweetheart. I need to feel your beautiful pussy wrapped around my cock."

I jumped up on my knees, my belly quivering in anticipation. I couldn't wait to have my men inside me, their cum mixing with my juices.

I crawled over Scott's beautiful lean body, kissing his tight abs and tiny pink nipples on the way up to his lips. My tortured hero was giving me his heart, his body, his future. I was so lucky.

"God, you're divine." Scott's words floated over me as he groaned and grabbed my waist, encouraging me to straddle him.

We'd never really discussed my weight before, so I threw it out there for one final reassurance. "You don't mind that I'm so...big?"

I glanced down at the rolls on my belly and then back at Scott, whose eyes were wide.

Then he said, "Are you fucking kidding me? I love how big you are! Sexiest woman on the planet as far as I'm concerned. You're gonna make beautiful, healthy babies, and your body turns me on more than any woman I've ever met."

I gaped at him. I knew Jack usually liked smaller women, but I didn't know about Scott's natural predilection. "Really?"

He grabbed my hand and wrapped it around his rock-hard cock. "Sweetheart, this is the best lie detector in the world. He's telling you that you're the hottest, sexiest, most beautiful woman in the world. So, hop on."

I laughed with pure happiness as I rubbed my wet pussy along the length of his cock. I ached so much for him. I needed him inside of me. I needed both of them.

I leaned forward and pressed a kiss to Scott's lips, tilted my pelvis, and moved until I'd positioned the head of his cock at the entrance to my pussy. I made direct eye contact with my beautiful scientist and slid down, encompassing his cock in one smooth movement.

"God, I love you..." I let my eyes close as my body was filled with his hard, thick flesh.

He groaned, arching his back and thrusting up as he dug his fingers into my hips. "I love you too."

Jack's large hands slid down my spine and nudged me forward. "Can you lean down and kiss Scott, honey?"

They're both going to be inside me soon. Oh, God...

With as much excitement as trepidation, I complied with his request, ignoring any niggling fear that surfaced in my mind.

They hadn't spelled it out to me, but when Scott had said they both needed to be inside me, I could only imagine one scenario where that would work.

I'd done it before, but under sufferance, and it hadn't gone well.

I was sure this time would be different. This time, I wanted it as well as the men and I trusted them not to hurt me.

I leaned forward and pressed my lips to Scott's, gasping against his mouth as Jack's fingers pressed lube against my ass.

"Oh, God." I moaned and concentrated on Scott's tongue flicking against mine, his hands on my back, distracting me.

A single finger pressed into my ass and I moaned against the burn, forcing myself to relax my muscles and press back to encourage Jack's intimacy.

Scott moved his hands around my waist and gripped my hips. He began moving faster inside me, thrusting up into my pussy and making Jack's fingers feel good as they slid against the cock inside me.

Jack added another finger, and then scissored them, stretching me as he pressed deep. He didn't stop until I was burning with need for him to be inside me too.

"Oh, God." I groaned and thrust against them.

It was all too much.

My clit throbbed and ached, so I ground myself down on Scott to receive some stimulation. Hot tingles sizzled around my pussy.

"Ready to take both of us, sweetheart?" Jack's voice behind me was a welcome relief from the frustration clawing through my belly.

I pushed up and away from Scott, nodding, and then gasped as Scott reached between us and pressed his fingers to my clit.

"Yes! Please!"

Hurry! Before I come.

Jack pushed his cock against my ass and I pressed back, rocking between my two men. I gasped as Jack's cock slipped deep inside me. "Oh. My. God."

I'd never been so full, so amazingly complete, yet crazily aroused. The fire burned hotter as my men pinned me between them. The conduit for their love and the center of their new family.

My men made guttural noises as they grabbed my body and began thrusting. Over and over they slid into me, turning me into a primitive being that could barely think, only feel.

They made me scream, cry out, and groan. I couldn't control the noises coming out of my mouth as they pumped harder and faster.

Everywhere they touched caused pleasure to ricochet through my body, sensations boiling up and consuming me.

My orgasm crashed down on me out of nowhere and I screamed,

my belly clamping down and exploding shards of ecstasy through my whole body.

My men moved within me in a perfect counter rhythm and my eyes slid shut, unable to stay open while lights went off like fireworks in my head.

"Fuck! I can't hold on anymore, I'm gonna come," Jack cried out from behind me.

Scott groaned beneath me, the air around us getting hotter by the minute. "Me, too."

They exploded inside meat the same time, the pulsing of their hot seed pushing me straight into another orgasm of mind-blowing intensity.

They continued, rolling on and on. The world spun and all sound disappeared into the darkness. My womb tightened and spasmed as Scott's cum filled me while Jack's warmth spread into me from behind.

Jack pressed himself to my back and bit into my right shoulder, and Scott lifted up and sank his teeth into the left.

My orgasm continued while my men bound me to them, their marks branding my skin...my heart...my soul...for all time.

Finally, the heated cloud around us stilled. Both men pulled out gently, and I gasped from the intense ache it caused.

Damn... I know they have to leave, but I miss it already.

"Stay here, baby." Scott pulled me down onto his sweaty chest and Jack disappeared. A moment later, he returned with a wet cloth.

He lay down on the bed next to us and crooned how beautiful I was as he cleaned between my legs.

I tried to properly open my eyes, but I couldn't get them to work. My eyelids fluttered and lights flickered, a blissful haze descending and dragging me down.

Scott moved me onto the mattress, arranging me between my perfect pair, and then a blanket was pulled up and the heat of their bodies pressed into me.

Their breath surrounded me, their words in my ears.

"I love you," they whispered to me in turn.

Love swelled inside me, and I nestled closer. "Oh…I love you both, too."

They were my perfect pair. Everything I'd ever wanted, needed, and dreamed of. All in one perfect package.

EPILOGUE

ASH

I waved my arms, wiggled my bum, and danced over to the large group of female cousins I'd invited to my wedding.

I'd gone out of my way to invite every one of my single cousins to the party. After Laura had found her men, and now me, I was convinced there was something special about our bloodline and the perfect pairs within Jack and Scott's family.

There were two unmarried twin sets at the reception, and I hoped to help them find their women, too.

"Samantha! Oh, my gosh, it's so good to see you!" I embraced my younger cousin from White Horse, Northern Canada. Sam hugged me back, squeezing tightly. "It's been so long since I saw you."

I pulled back, and she smiled up at me. "I know, but how could I resist your demand of us single girls coming down for a party?"

I laughed as Sam wiggled her large hips from side to side. She was by far the shortest and plumpest of us all, but I had discovered that, for these men, that meant nothing.

If anything, our size seemed to set us apart; make us special in our perfect pairs' eyes.

"Yeah, thanks for an amazing night," Sam said.

The women around us gave me kisses and congratulations, before continuing to dance and sing to the music.

I joined in the fun, but my gaze kept swinging back to Sam. There was something about her that I had never fully appreciated before. A glow, a vibrancy. Could she possibly be the perfect mate for another perfect pair?

Someone moved up behind me, and I twisted as Jack wrapped his arms around my waist. His hands slid down to the curve of my hip and ass in a familiar and possessive way.

"Hello, husband." I beamed and slid my arms around his thick neck and strong shoulders.

I still couldn't believe I was officially mated to not only two men, but two mountain lion shifter men. My scientific brain was well and truly blown. Would wonders never cease?

"Hello, wife." He swooped in and kissed me, pulling me even closer against his solidness.

I let him seduce my body as my heart sang. His lips were soft and persistent, his hands caring and protective. I was so lucky.

Eventually, he pulled away. "Can you come with me for a minute?"

"Of course." I let myself be pulled away to the tree next to the patio, where Scott stood with two rather somber-looking gentlemen in full black attire.

Scott took my hand and indicated to the men beside him. "Ash, these are our cousins from up north, Kane and Reid. This is our wife and mate, Ashleigh."

Both men nodded and gave me matching smiles that looked more like grimaces. I only just prevented my recoil. Why did they look so unhappy?

"It's lovely to meet you both," I managed.

"Hi."

I stepped a little closer to Jack, and Scott moved to my other side, kissing my bare shoulder in a soothing gesture. There was something unsettling about this pair of brothers, and I wasn't sure what it was.

Scott rubbed his hand up and down my arm. "Sweetheart, can you tell us about the little brunette you were just talking to?"

I stared at Scott, and then at the men across from me. There was only one reason Scott would ask me this question.

They were another perfect pair.

They looked very similar to my husbands, in a way.

One light, one dark.

One slightly shorter and thinner, the other one tall and built like a tree trunk.

"You mean Samantha?" I turned and watched my cousin shimmy away on the dance floor.

"Yeah, the shorter, curvy one." Jack smiled at me, his gaze alight as he squeezed my ass through my dress.

I bumped him with my hip and grinned back. I was happy to say that my insecurities had faded into non-existence. My men loved my body and as they healed my scars, I healed theirs.

The fated mate bond was a wonderful, beautiful thing for all of us.

I focused back on the question. "Sam is great. She's twenty-nine, a schoolteacher. Single, fun, opinionated, and has the biggest heart in the world. Why?"

I looked at the men before me, their faces pale and generally unhealthy-looking. Were they both unwell?

Scott continued, his voice gentle. "Kane and Reid feel a connection to her, and we were wondering about her, that's all."

One of the men stepped back suddenly, color finally rising in his pale cheeks. "This is ridiculous. Our mate died, Scott. It can't be true."

I gasped. *Oh, no! You poor men! How could fate be so cruel?*

Scott stepped toward Kane, reaching out for him. "But you shouldn't still be alive, Kane. It doesn't make sense. Perhaps you were...mistaken. Before."

Reid stepped back too and pulled Kane away from Scott. "Impossible! Kellie was perfect for us."

Scott lifted his hands in a gesture of peace. "I'm not saying she wasn't. Maybe Fate designed you two mates, knowing you'd lose Kellie early? I don't know, but if you're still alive and feeling the connection again, why wouldn't you chase it? Jack and I did, and it was the best decision of our lives."

Jack pulled me tighter. I smiled and let the love flow between our connection, warming me and acknowledging the rightness of everything in my life.

"I hope you never know how this feels, Scott. It's…" Kane's voice broke.

My heart ached as the two men turned and stumbled away with gentle growls emanating from their obviously broken hearts.

"Those poor men," I said, shaking my head. "What happened to them? They look like a perfect pair. Their mate died?"

Jack wrapped his big arms around me. "Yes, sweetheart, she did."

I gripped Jack tightly and reached out for Scott. I couldn't think of anything worse.

"I don't think I'd survive without you two now," I said. "You're my whole world."

My men pressed close, their lips in my hair, their hands and arms protecting me and the unborn child that my mates still didn't know about.

I smiled at the secret that I would share with them soon.

Jack whispered in my ear. "We'll never leave you, sweetheart, and if you left us, we'd soon join you."

"Pardon me?" That better not have been some sort of promise to die if I wasn't here. "You better not mean that, Jack."

I pulled back for some much-needed air.

Scott cupped my jaw. "It's not something we can control, gorgeous. When a mate dies, the perfect pair usually die of natural causes within twelve months, which is why I don't believe Kane and Reid lost their true mate. They wouldn't be here if she had been."

My head spun with too much new information. "Are you telling me that if I die, it'll kill you guys too? That can't be! Please, you can't do that."

Why hadn't they told me that?

Hot, salty tears streamed down my face, and Jack swung me up in his arms. He walked us inside our new house, only stopping when we were finally sitting on our new bed. Scott was right behind us.

Scott pulled me tighter toward him, cuddling me on the bed. "What's wrong, Ash? Please don't cry."

I couldn't help it, the pain in my chest was almost crushing me. I couldn't breathe. "That's horrible! I can't handle that. We can't— what about the baby? How would they survive without us? How?"

I could feel how unreasonable I was becoming as the hiccuping and tears overtook my ability to talk.

Bloody hormones! Calm down. The men chuckled and cuddled me on the bed, their noises soothing and lovely.

"Honey, firstly, we don't expect any of us to die until we are all old and gray, and...*wait*. Did you just say...*baby*?" Scott's voice rose as Jack let out a delighted gasp.

I grabbed at the tissues Jack handed me and blotted at my face that I was sure no longer resembled a woman who'd spent two hours having wedding makeup applied.

"Yes, I did! I found out last week and wanted to surprise you," I said, between sobs. "But now you've got me all freaked out about dying."

My men laughed and jumped on me, rolling me around in the beautiful big bed that was meant for our wedding night.

Scott cupped my face, love for me shining through his beautiful green eyes. "So, we really are going to have the family we always dreamed of."

His fingers spread over my belly.

I nodded, gripping Jack's hand in one of mine. "Yes, we are."

We'd had a family picnic the week before and I'd had lunch with all five future stepchildren. They'd all spoken to me, though it had been stilted at times.

Even Meaghan had smiled once or twice, and I'd somehow managed to stay upright from the glares I copped from both ex-wives. It wasn't going to be an easy road, but we were on the way.

I sighed and focused on the three of us. My men weren't the only ones whose dreams were about to come true.

At thirty-five and divorced, I'd been convinced my life was over. But now I had men who loved me, and we'd created a baby I knew we would all adore.

No fantasy I'd ever created could hold a candle to the reality that was now my life.

THE END

~

Book 3 in the series is available to buy:
https://books2read.com/shadowingtheirmate

Read on for a sneak peek into 'Shadowing their Mate'...

~

I reached over and squeezed my twin brother's forearm, as much for Reid's benefit as my own. "Breathe, Reid, just breathe. There has to be an explanation for this."

I sucked some much-needed oxygen into my lungs, my heart hammering hard enough against my ribs to make my stomach lurch. Streams of adrenaline were pulsing through my weakened body, making lights dance at the edges of my vision.

"But ... she can't be, Kane. You know she can't. What the hell is this?" Reid demanded.

I have no fucking idea.

I didn't want to admit to my twin that I was at as big a loss as him, and since Reid was freaking out, it had fallen on me to find out what was happening.

I tried one more time. "Seriously, Reid, there has to be a rational explanation for this. Just calm down." I squeezed my twin's forearm and stood up.

This tingling, excited feeling that was infiltrating both me and my perfect pair brother was scary. It was the opposite of what we'd expected when we came to visit our family for Jack and Scott's bonding ceremony with Ashleigh.

Our purpose had been to say goodbye to everyone. We'd waited out the first year of our grief, expecting an illness or something similar to set in. The legends had foretold our deaths, but not the how or why.

"Hey, guys. Enjoying the party?"

I turned toward the sound of Jack's voice, one of the grooms and our cousin on our mother's side.

I forced a smile to my face. "Yes, we are. Thanks for the invitation, Jack. And congratulations again. You seem very happy."

Reid stood and now loomed silently beside me. I straightened my spine against the cold wave that wafted toward me. Reid had lost all warmth and emotion in the past year, and it was creepy that I barely recognized my twin. He was merely a shell of the man he used to be.

Jack grinned and slapped me on the arm, the strength of the blow enough to make my shoes slip on the grass.

Jack steadied me with a wink. It was strange to think Reid had once been as big as the mountain that Jack was. "Sorry, bud. Yeah, we're ecstatic. It was great that you were able to make it."

I smiled at my cousin's happy demeanor, but I was still very aware of my brother being eerily silent beside me.

"We were glad to make it. Reid and I have both taken leaves of absence from work and haven't given a date to go back."

Which was mostly because we'd expected to be dead by now.

Thirteen months, twenty-one days. But who's counting?

Jack's twin, Scott, walked up and shook our hands. "So glad you both made it."

Reid cleared his throat with painful, rough purring sounds. "Kane, I think we should go."

I squashed the growl that rose in response to my brother's suggestion that we leave without finding out about the woman on the dance floor.

Whoa, a growl? Really?

I hadn't shifted in over a year and hadn't sensed my lion anywhere inside me. One disagreement with my twin and my shifter was back? Doubtful.

Was it the woman calling to my lion?

I tilted my head toward the call of the siren. "Can either of you tell us who is the woman dancing with your wife?"

As a group, we turned to look over at the stage where Ashleigh waved her arms, wiggled her ass, and danced with a group of women. She had been talking earlier to the brunette that both Reid and I felt a connection to, and now they were laughing and hugging each other.

Scott's voice moved closer. "Why do you ask, Kane? Are you feeling something?"

I weighed my options and lying was one of them. I opened my mouth and the only possible answer came out. "Yeah, we both do. Not sure what it is, but we'd like to find out before we head home."

"*You* might," Reid's voice was gruff next to me.

I turned and glared at my twin. We were both living in hell these days anyway. What difference did it make if we turned the heat up a notch?

"I'll go get her," Jack said as he brushed past me, moving toward the dance floor, then embracing his beautiful bride as he got within arm's length of the woman I was so curious about.

Ashleigh absolutely glowed with happiness as Jack kissed her and talked to her with a love that was obviously returned.

Tendrils of envy and stabbing sadness wove through me as I watched them. My shoulders were aching with tension, and my throat was too tight to swallow. My eyes wandered away from the lovebirds to where the brunette was chatting and dancing, my stomach clenching in strange waves of unease. She was very, *very* beautiful. There was no other word for the aura of light and happiness she emitted.

Finally, the big football player pulled his bride away from the stage and joined us once again. "Ash, these are our cousins from up north, Kane and Reid. This is our wife and mate, Ashleigh."

I smiled at Jack and Scott's wife, her skin glowing in the well-lit area.

"It's lovely to meet you both." She smiled back at us, and I stumbled in my attempt to greet her.

"Hi."

Reid coughed and nodded his head. "Yes, you, too."

Ashleigh stepped a little closer to Jack and Scott, who both moved as if to comfort her, kissing her bare shoulders in a soothing gesture. She seemed skittish now, and it pained me to see it.

We really must present worse than I thought if this beautiful woman showed signs of discomfort in our presence. But then again, when was the last time I'd looked in a mirror?

Scott spoke to his wife with a gentle voice. "Sweetheart, can you tell us about the little brunette you were talking to just now?"

Ashleigh stared up at Scott as he asked her the question, then looked at Reid and me with her eyebrows raised.

"You mean Samantha?" Ashleigh turned her head and they all followed suit, watching the group of women on the dance floor. They were all lovely and young, but the woman I was asking about kept drawing my gaze like a moth to a flame.

"Yeah, the shorter, curvy one." Jack grinned at Ashleigh and I frowned. Was she? I had another good look at the woman my cousin's wife called Samantha. She *was* shorter and more voluptuous than the women around her. I hadn't really noticed initially.

Ashleigh bumped Jack with her hip and smiled back at him.

"Sam's great. She's twenty-nine, a schoolteacher, who lives about two hours from here. Single, fun, opinionated, and has the biggest heart in the world. Why?"

She was younger than I'd thought, but the rest all sounded good. Not that I was interested in anything past finding out what the strange feeling my twin and I were experiencing, of course.

"Kane and Reid feel a connection to her, and we were wondering about her, that's all."

Scott added, "Actually, honey, I think it might be a good idea to introduce them."

Scott turned to wink at me and horror flooded through my chest like a sudden storm, drenching my skin in adrenaline-induced sweat. My cousin couldn't be thinking that we were interested in Samantha for anything more than knowledge?

"I hope you're not implying what I think you are, Scott. Our mate died. We don't need to meet another woman."

Scott stepped toward me, his face full of concern and worry. I was sick and tired of those expressions from everyone around us.

"But you shouldn't be alive still," Scott said gently. "Kane, it doesn't make sense. Perhaps you were... mistaken."

I stumbled away as pain made my muscles tremble and weaken so I could barely stand. Reid stepped back even further, pulling at my shoulder as though to get me away from Scott.

"No! Kellie was perfect for us!" I yelled back at him.

The tension of the group was making Jack growl and grab Ashleigh, pulling her behind him. My own body began to ripple with the warmth of pending transformation, and I took a deep breath to calm my heart. I couldn't possibly shift while holding onto this much grief. It was impossible.

Scott stepped forward again, his hands up and out as though he were offering a peaceful entreaty. "I'm not saying she wasn't. Maybe Fate designed you two mates, knowing you'd lose Kellie early on? I don't know, but if you are still alive and feeling a connection again, why wouldn't you chase it? Jack and I did, despite all the shit we went through, and it was the best decision of our lives."

I shook my head and continued to move backwards. Away from the painful promise my cousin's words evoked, and the fear that consumed my every thought.

"I hope you never know how this feels, Scott. It's..." My voice broke and I turned away, pulling my brother with me. I tried to be the strong and calm one, but today I'd failed miserably.

I moved fast through the crowd and finally stepped into fresh air, the path to our car now a clear one.

Today had been a mistake. Why had we thought that coming to another perfect pair wedding was a good idea? Jack and Scott were just as happy as we had been on our wedding day with Kellie. Seeing them all together and glowing with love was enough to make my heart ache. But to feel tendrils of life again at seeing Samantha was too much to bear.

"Let's go back to the motel." Reid took out his car keys, opened our rental and jumped in.

I grabbed at the door handle and let my eyes lift up to see the lights still flickering through the trees surrounding the reception and the guests.

"I wish it were true, Scott. But it's just not possible."

I let my voice drift toward my cousin, where he stood out of earshot, still at the party.

I got into the car and let Reid drive us away. From our family, from the bridal party, and the woman who'd made me feel more alive than I had in more than a year.

Samantha

"I can't believe you're married to *two* men, Ash!" I playfully pushed at my beautiful cousin, shaking my head at the unusual situation. "And Laura, too!"

There was obviously something strange going on around here, and it looked contagious.

Ashleigh laughed and fluttered her eyelashes at me, her sparkling eyes a testament to how happy she was. "Well, I can tell you, it works ten times better than any other relationship I've ever had."

I giggled, noting for the first time the healthy glow to my cousin's face. "I'm sure they keep you very well satisfied."

Ashleigh burst out laughing and linked our arms, pulling me so that we could walk away from the group. "We're heading off on our honeymoon on Monday," Ash said. "Otherwise I would have loved to spend more time with you. You need to come back for a longer visit next time."

I smiled and nodded. "Totally agree. I managed to take the week off, so I'm going to do some sightseeing and relaxing while I'm here. Catch up with Laura, too."

I needed a vacation more than anything, and catching up with my cousins had been a great excuse to get away from work.

I was looking forward to seeing how Laura was coping with being pregnant and working full time still. Though I was pretty sure that having two husbands on hand would make a pretty big difference.

Ash squeezed my arm tightly. "Oh, that's great! Maybe you could stay at our place for the week? Have you made reservations yet?"

I smiled at my generous cousin. "I've booked for the week but haven't paid yet."

"Brilliant! Then you can house-sit for us! Are you coming to the barbecue tomorrow? We're having all the family over for lunch."

I smiled and grabbed Ashleigh's hands in my own, my cousin squeezing back tightly. "I'll be there with bells on. But are you sure, Ash? I'd hate to put you out like that."

Ashleigh shook her head. "Not at all. I don't want you cooped up in a hotel room when you could have the run of our new place. Do you know how to get there?"

"I think someone gave me the address. It should be in my phone." I hoped it was, anyway. The navigation system in my rental would get me there.

"Great. Jack and Scott used to live separately and they've kept those houses and rented them out. We bought a new home over near Laura, actually. It's got a huge backyard, perfect for entertaining."

I pulled Ashleigh in for a tight hug, love for my cousin pouring through me like warm honey. "I am so happy for you, hon. You deserve to be happy after everything you've been through."

Even if it's with two, older, hunky men, which is just plain weird.

I'd never liked Ashleigh's ex-husband. I'd tried for the sake of my cousin to get along with the jerk, but every time I saw him, he just gave me the creeps. The stories of his emotional abuse of Ash made my hair stand on end.

Ashleigh pulled back and gave me a contented smile. "No more than you deserve to be happy, Sam. I hope you find the man—or men —for you very soon."

I burst out laughing. "Men? Me? Why? Does your pair have another set of brothers I should meet?"

That'd be the day! I could barely hold the interest of one man, let alone two.

Ashleigh tilted her head. "No, not brothers exactly, but they've got some cousins I'd love you to meet."

I let my hands drop away from Ashleigh's, my smile falling from my face.

I hadn't thought about the possibility of my family trying to set me up with anyone. No one knew about my boyfriend of almost a year. I hadn't introduced Bill to anyone yet, but that was my choice. I didn't need everyone knowing my personal business. But it would have stopped this happening.

"No, I don't need a fix up. Please don't."

"What do you mean? You're so gorgeous any guy would be ecstatic to have you!"

I groaned and rolled my eyes. "Ash, really. I'm fine just the way I am."

Ashleigh's gaze fell away in obvious disappointment, and I reeled in my patience. "Look, I understand that you're just trying to help, but I'm happy."

Ashleigh smiled kindly and cocked her head. "Well, come to the lunch tomorrow anyway, and I'll introduce you to Jack and Scott's family. They're all lovely. You'll have a good time no matter what, I'm sure."

Yeah, I know I will.

I'd have Laura and Ash to talk to, and there were a few other cousins I was looking forward to seeing again, too. I turned as people began approaching the bride and decided to make my exit. A song I loved had just come over the speakers, and I began bouncing on the spot in time with the music.

"I better get back to your party. Congratulations again! You really are the most beautiful bride I've ever seen."

Ashleigh flushed pink and gave me a coy smile. "Thanks, Sam."

A couple of her in-laws grabbed Ashleigh, so I turned and sashayed my way back to the dance floor. I was happy as I was, loud, big-assed, and proud of it. Well, mostly happy.

I was a good person and I had a lot to offer someone. I had a boyfriend, but I knew he wasn't the one. Hopefully one day I'd find a man who could love me for all my faults as well as my assets.

DOWNLOAD BOOK 3: HERE